To Brian

MW01012452

DARK
BLOOD
COMES FROM
THE FEET

Emma J. Gibbon

Emma J. Gibbon

TREPIDATIO
PUBLISHING

Copyright 2020 © Emma J. Gibbon

All rights reserved. No part of this book may be used or reproduced by any means, graphic, electronic, or mechanical, including photocopying, recording, taping or by any information storage retrieval system without the written permission of the publisher except in the case of brief quotations embodied in critical articles and reviews.

This is a work of fiction. All of the characters, names, incidents, organizations, and dialogue in this novel are either the products of the author's imagination or are used fictitiously.

The views expressed in this work are solely those of the authors and do not necessarily reflect the views of the publisher, and the publisher hereby disclaims any responsibility for them.

ISBN: 978-1-950305-28-5 (sc)
ISBN: 978-1-950305-29-2 (ebook)
Library of Congress Control Number: 2020937917

First printing edition: May 22, 2020
Published by Trepidatio Publishing in the United States of America.
Cover Design and Layout: Don Noble
Interior Layout and Editing: Scarlett R. Algee
Proofread by Sean Leonard
Author Photo by Teri Schultz

Trepidatio Publishing, an imprint of JournalStone Publishing
3205 Sassafras Trail
Carbondale, Illinois 62901

Trepidatio books may be ordered through booksellers or by contacting:
Trepidatio | www.trepidatio.com
or
JournalStone | www.journalstone.com

For Steve, who always knows who I am.

DARK BLOOD

BLOOD

COMES FROM

THE FEET

THE LIMBO LOUNGE

We had a hard time convincing the new girl, even after she'd been here for a while. "Ever notice that you never sleep?" we'd say. "Never eat? Never leave? Can you remember the last time you went home?"

"I can remember," she'd say. "You're just messing with me," and she would blink those big blue eyes at us, made bigger by those sparkly fake eyelashes that she always wore. She strapped on her towering platform high heels and strode out through the glitter curtain onto the stage for her next dance. We'd look at each other, roll our perfectly made-up eyes, and get ready for our number.

We all have our favorite songs that we dance to. Except we don't choose them, exactly. When we walk through the glitter curtain, they just start playing. The song she gets the most is "Unskinny Bop." I'd have thought that song would have been way too old for her. Surely she wasn't even born in the 80s? But she told me her mom had really loved it and had played it when she was a kid. Maybe I'm old enough now to be her mother...or would have been.

I guess the songs are whatever sticks. The song I get the most is "You Give Love a Bad Name." I suppose that's about my vintage. I lost my virginity to that album. That young fresh girl in cut-off jeans in the backseat of a car is a long way from the woman who ended up here. Juniper still has deep purple track marks down her arms. It plays "Glory Box" when she goes out. She still cries every time she dances. Roberta's song is "Bad Reputation." Monique's is "Hypnotize." That's a good one.

There's so many of us here. We get to hear all the stripper hits: "Girls, Girls, Girls," "Cherry Pie," "American Woman," a lot of Britney and Christina Aguilera. Sometimes we get girls now that dance to songs that are after our time. The years go by out there, even if they don't in here. We learn the lyrics, though. It's a nice change of pace.

We have to make the new girl understand where she is. It's part of our job. If we don't, well, she'll go to the other place. Below. And that means we've failed. It's only happened once since I got here, but I've heard the stories, and well, once is enough.

Sherry was perfect. Strawberry blonde curls down her back, the longest legs I'd ever seen. I don't remember ever seeing her eyes. She always wore those heart-shaped sunglasses that were popular when I was a kid. Her song was "Sweet Child O' Mine." She refused to believe. Straight up refused. We tried to explain to her, point out the discrepancies, just like we always do with the new girl. "When was the last time you saw the sun?" we'd say. "Can you remember the last time you drove to work? Do you remember the last time you ate? Slept in your own bed?"

"Yes," she would say, lying through her teeth. "I remember all of those things. Y'all crazy." She used her pinky finger to make sure her fire-engine red lipstick hadn't smudged. It would never smudge. "As soon as my shift is over, I'm gone. I'm taking my tips. I ain't sharing with you loons and I'm getting out of here. There's plenty of strip joints in this town where I can get work. I can walk in anywhere."

"Do you remember what this place is called?" we'd say. "Don't you think it's funny that you can never see the customers' faces? They're sort of blurry, right? But, they don't seem to change, go home." She'd shake her head. "Y'all crazy," she'd repeat. We'd get indignant. "Where's the money, Sherry? Where's all the money they gave you for your last stage dance? Disappeared like vapor, like it always does."

Sherry huffed and pouted. "One of you bitches stole it, probably. After this shift, I'm out. Y'all can kiss my ass goodbye." But, of course, she remained. She was steadfast, though, until that very last shift. Monique was the one who saw it first. She nudged me with her elbow.

"She's starting to go," she said. We knew it was too late. She was turning black around the edges, like burnt paper, and you could detect the scent of sulfur following her. Still, we tried. "Honey," said Monique, "you just have to say it. Say you know where you are and maybe you won't go to the other place."

"I'm not your honey," said Sherry, and that was when her face caved in.

Then that noise, like high winds outside the house at night or a jet engine setting off, and she was gone. Gone through the dance floor like she was never here, a black soot stain on the tile was all that remained. Roberta grabbed the mop and wiped it up.

Now the new girl. Still not believing. Still in jeopardy. There's always the option of going up, of course, and I always hope for it for all the girls that come here. I've never seen it happen, although sometimes people are just gone and I have to hope that they've gone up instead of down. What is absolutely certain, though: If you don't recognize you're here, then you're going down.

We're getting ready to go on the floor. We're in the dressing room. We go through the actions of putting on makeup, but that's more out of habit. It stays on. We're just going through the motions. These are our faces now. The new girl is talking about her plans. How when she's saved up enough tips, she and her boyfriend are going to get out of this town, going to Hollywood, trying their luck. Juniper loses her temper, her track marks glowing ultraviolet under the vanity lights. "You're fucking dead," she says. "Have you not fucking noticed that yet? Why do you think we keep asking you these dumb questions? You're never going to Hollywood. The boyfriend is gone. The sooner you let that sink in, the easier it will be for all of us."

The new girl blinks, twice, draws herself to her full height, still only five foot six in those stacked heels. "Why do you have to be so negative, Juniper?" She pushes past us and strides out, swishing through the glitter curtains, and gives the performance of her death. Her song plays louder than ever before. We watch from the wings, open-mouthed. She glides and swings around the pole, swoops and soars, appears to dance on air. Her skin is shimmery, luminous. She looks like a goddamn angel. Those blurry figures, the customers that are always there, always not, throw money at her. Dollar bills fly though the air like the whole club is one of those "Grab a Fortune" machines and there are so many coins on the floor it looks like it's paved in gold. We've never seen anything like it. We all cheer and clap when she's done.

I find her crying in the bathroom later, in mascara that never runs. She tells me she knows where she is. "I'm stuck here forever, right?" she says.

"Probably," I say.

PORCH

I live in the woods. Not like in a fairy tale. Not some witchy cottage down a dark path, but a clean, airy trailer on a wooded lot. It's the boonies, but not in the middle of nowhere. I have neighbors, a paved road nearby. I don't know why that matters, but I just want you to know that. My cat, Rufus, is big and black with wide, gleaming green eyes. When the light hits his fur, it has a brownish-reddish tinge, like he was left out in the rain for too long and rusted. He was supposed to be an inside cat. I promised the shelter, but you know how these things go. He was forever pleading to go out, escaping every chance he got. He's just happier when he gets to go outside. I know there are things out there that could hurt him. I'm a bad cat owner.

It's just me and Rufus who live here. There was a man once, some years ago, but he left. I loved him, I think. He was tall and kind and gentle, but we did not understand each other. "I feel like you don't need me," he said. I tried to tell him, show him how much I did need him, want him, but he left anyway, got involved with someone at work. I don't mind being alone. I mean, I'm not, really. Rufus is good company and I talk to people. I make soap and sell it online, so I talk to the people at the store, at the post office. I got some money from a household mold case when I was younger, so I do okay. I live quietly. I expect it to be just me and Rufus for quite some time. I've heard people talk about "magic animals," like pet soulmates, I suppose. I don't know about that, but Rufus has felt more like a life partner than any other being I've known. I wonder if in the past I'd have been burnt at the stake for having a familiar. I probably would have been burnt at the stake for a lot of things.

I can't remember exactly the first time Rufus brought me one of his gifts. It was spring. It was a tiny mouse. I heard Rufus scratch at the screen and went to let him in. He was sitting on the porch, the small animal laid in front of the step like a small offering. Rufus looked up at me and blinked his big lamplight eyes. "Oh, Rufus," I said, "the poor thing." I assumed it was dead. There was no overt physical evidence of a mauling, but when I looked closely, it had a trickle of blood coming from its mouth. "Rufus," I said, "how could you!" But then the little thing twitched, making me jump. A film of sickening sweat covered my skin. I couldn't stand the tiny creature suffering, but back then I just didn't have the guts to finish it off. I knew other people hit things with a shovel. It's not that I wasn't physically capable. I'm a strong and sturdy woman, despite not being very outdoorsy. It was the thought of the tiny thing in pain that made my gorge rise. I didn't even know if I had a shovel—maybe in the shed? Why couldn't Rufus have finished the poor thing off? I looked at Rufus. He blinked again, yawned, showing his carnivore teeth. I knew cats did this. He thought I was a big, dumb, hairless cat who couldn't hunt and needed help. Maybe he was right.

I dashed inside, bile bubbling in my throat. I googled what to do. It was a mess of conflicting advice. I had no gun. I already knew I wasn't going to decapitate or crush the head. Some mentioned asphyxiation with a jar. In the end, I took the coward's way out. Let nature take its course, the forums said. It's natural. Put it outside to die. I scooped the mouse into my hands and carried its quickly cooling body to the tree line. "I'm sorry," I whispered to it. "This is my fault. I put a predator in your midst." Rufus followed me. I thought he was judging me for rejecting his gift. I laid the mouse on the ground, gave him a bed of old leaves. "I'm sorry," I said to him again. "Sleep tight, die fast, no more pain." I put a saucer of water next to it, just in case a miracle happened. I walked back to the trailer, my heart crushed, not daring to look back. Rufus followed me, meowing plaintively.

I talked to Judy at the store the next day. I still had not gone to the part of the yard where I had deposited the mouse. I'd not slept well. It haunted me. Judy was unconcerned. "It's just what cats do. It's their nature. Especially in spring," she said. "Besides, mice are pests. Maybe Rufus should come and stay with me for a while. My barn is overrun." She laughed and then coughed a smoker's rasp. I knew I was probably overreacting. I lived in the country, after all. I needed to toughen up.

"If you do this again," I said to Rufus as I filled his bowl with cat food, "you'll have to become an indoor cat again." But I knew I couldn't do it to him. He was just so much happier being free to roam outside.

A miracle hadn't happened. When I plucked up the courage to return to the mouse, it was stiff and cold. I used a trowel to dig a little grave by the oak trees and asked for his body to nourish the soil.

I tried to preempt Rufus after that. I scanned the yard for animals before I let him out, and even shouted: "Get out of the way! Save yourselves!" The squirrels scampered up the trees at the sound of my voice.

It didn't work, of course. A couple of weeks later, spring almost over: A vole, breathing quick and fast on my porch, its back end mangled. "Why?" I said to Rufus. He sat cleaning his paws. I knew I couldn't carry it away again, thinking about it all night. So I grabbed a glass jar from the recycling and placed the vole inside, screwing the lid tight. I didn't stay to watch it expire. The internet said that it was one of the kindest things to do. I left it on the step to deal with in the morning. I prayed to whatever vole-god existed to take this child to a better place, quickly. The next morning, when I was sure it was dead, I buried it next to the mouse.

That wasn't the end of it, of course. It never is, is it? I had been set down a course. Rufus had a plan, and I had to follow it. I ended up doing things I said I wouldn't or couldn't do. Everything is always that simple, and always that difficult, always.

The first thing I was wrong about was that it didn't end in spring. I'd heard that cats tended to get some kind of spring fever, but as the heat rose and summer took over, his behavior didn't change. He continued bringing gifts. The second thing that I was wrong about was that Rufus was the one who was doing the deed. I had thought that he was bringing me his not-quite-completed kills. That might have been the case, at first, but as time went on and he started bringing me bigger things, it became clear that he was collecting them rather than simply maiming them: the squirrel with an infected leg, the rabbit mauled by something much bigger than Rufus, a young cat run over by a car, a small, old, white-muzzled dog, its body full of tumors.

I tried to save them at first. I drove the little squirrel to a wildlife rehabilitator in the next town. She gave her antibiotics and painkillers and a heating pad to lie on. She covered her in diatomaceous earth to get rid of the fleas. The squirrel didn't make it through the night. The woman called me in the morning. "At least she died peacefully and painlessly," she said. "You did the right thing. I loved her until the end."

I tried not to cry when I told Judy at the store. She patted my arm and said it was a shame, but that's how things go, y'know?

I took the cat and the dog to the vet, tried to find their owners, but nothing. Nothing could be done. I paid to have them both put to sleep. I took them home with me and buried them in the yard. The thought of mass cremation upset me. The rehabilitator lady's words rang in my ears. Perhaps that was what Rufus meant me to do. Perhaps I couldn't save them, but I could be an angel of death to these poor creatures. Love them until the end. That night, Rufus lay across my chest, directly over my heart, and slept. It seemed like a sign that I was right.

It was fall. Rufus brought a raccoon, my favorite animal. I watched him drag it across the yard, praying that it would escape and run off into the woods. He was in bad shape, poor thing. I don't know how he had got into such a mess. His chest heaved. I knew he needed release. This time I was braver, but only because he kept his eyes closed. If he had looked up at me, I couldn't have done it. I grabbed the shovel that I'd bought from Home Depot on my last trip to town (telling myself I would do yard work—who I was kidding?). I swung it down and put the poor little guy out of its misery. It was the least I could do. Rufus seemed satisfied, and stalked inside while I buried the cooling body. This time, I didn't stop the tears falling. I cried and cried for that little raccoon and wondered if I had the strength to complete the task that Rufus had set me on.

There were more and more: a porcupine, a coyote, even a black bear cub. I would have never believed that Rufus could have brought them to my door if I hadn't seen it with my own eyes. He was big for a cat, but still. Some of them I never witnessed. I would hear his meow, and there he was at the door with his latest offering. More and more, his gifts were much bigger than himself.

I told Judy about it. She couldn't believe it either. "Clever Rufus," she said. "How on earth does he do it?" I thought about telling her that I was meant to euthanize them rather than save them. Tell her that Rufus was a deliverer, and that's how he could manage the seemingly impossible. But when I was getting bread, I saw Judy in the shoplifter mirror. She was whirling her finger around her temple, then pointing at me. "Crazy," I heard her stage whisper to another customer. I didn't bother talking to Judy after that.

I did go to another store in town, though. I bought a gun. I knew that the shovel wasn't going to do it. I lived in constant fear that I wouldn't hit my target true or hard enough. To cause more pain and suffering than necessary was unbearable to me. There were no jars big enough. I asked the man behind the counter to give me something powerful that was easy to use. "Not thinking about offing the old man?" he said, chuckling. I tried to smile, but I think I just bared my teeth.

"I don't have an old man," I said.

"Be careful with that," he said and handed me the gun.

"I'm always careful," I said, and tried to smile again.

I practiced shooting in the yard. Rufus watched from the tree stump. I told the neighbors I was having trouble with rats. We live in the country. It's what people do.

Of course there were more, bigger and bigger, a big old Maine Coon ailing from some disease, its fur matted and so thin that its legs looked like stalks; a starved Great Dane, scarred and tired; a deer with its back legs broken. I asked Rufus if he was sure; maybe they could be saved? But the way he blinked his big green eyes at me, I knew. I knew what he wanted me to do, what my role was, so I dispatched them all as quickly as I could. Tough calluses studded my hands from digging all the graves. Winter was coming.

So then, a reprieve: the weather got cold, very cold. Ice lined the driveway and the air was bitter in my lungs. We stayed in, going out as little as possible. Rufus stayed by the wood stove for the most part and I worked, making soaps, existing on the cans of food I had stashed away. I had kept the woodshed stocked. I went to the post office only when I had to, and bought necessities on the way back. I never went to Judy's store again. We hunkered down, reveling in the splendid isolation of winter.

But then came the storm.

Winter was almost over. It lingered, but the first breaths of spring were in the air, barely perceptible but there under the frost. That morning, Rufus had escaped through my legs as I went to the woodshed, and had run out into the trees. I was surprised that he would leave the warmth of the trailer, but took it as another sign that spring was nearly here.

It was a cold but bright day. I kept an eye out for him but didn't see him. I wasn't unduly worried, but that night a storm whipped up outside of the likes that we hadn't seen in years. The wind howled around the trailer, almost as if it would pick it up and carry it away like Dorothy's house. The rain was a deluge, cascading down the windows and walls. Out in the woods, I could hear the trees snapping and bending. I went out to the porch and shouted, "Rufus," over and over again, but there was no way he could hear me over the roar of the weather. Instead, I took vigil at the window and watched for him as the storm raged.

I sat there a long time, into the evening, past midnight. I jerked awake around 3 a.m., my cheek cold from the windowsill. The wind had died down and the rain had nearly stopped. I heard a familiar meow at the door. I knew he had brought something, but couldn't make out what it was through the wet, smudged glass. It was bigger than anything else he had brought before.

I opened the door, and there on the step was a man. Younger than me, perhaps early thirties, he was naked and lay on his side in a fetal position. He was soaked. His dark hair plastered to his pale, goose-fleshed skin. Rufus sat next to him, still as a statue. "Rufus, how on earth did you...?" The man was shivering hard, and I could see he was breathing but only shallowly, his chest slowly rising and falling. He turned his head to look at me and tried to speak, but I could tell he was having trouble forming words. His eyes then rolled back and he passed out. "Maybe we could save him, Rufus?" I implored. "Maybe this time is different." Rufus looked up at me steadily. He didn't blink this time, and I knew. I knew what I had to do. The same as I always had to do. I could argue with Rufus. I could argue with fate. I could try to argue with who and what I was, but there was no changing the outcome. Love them until the end. I placed the flat of my palm on the man's cool, clammy shoulder. He didn't respond. I went and got my gun, and I delivered him as I was supposed to do. The sun was just coming up, and I felt its warmth for the first time in months.

I confess it was a shallow grave I placed him in. The ground was not quite thawed, and he was bigger than all the others. In the end, I used leaves to cover him up completely. I would work out the rest later.

It was then that the miracle happened. I stood in my yard, soaked to the skin, my palms burning from the shovel. At once, the mice and the voles, the rabbit and the raccoon, the porcupine, the coyote, the cats and deer, the dogs and the bear, all the others crawled out of the holes I'd dug for them. All of them were whole and healthy and vibrant in the cold morning air. They were resurrected and complete. I stood agog, Rufus at my side, as they all ran in different directions, escaping back into life. I crouched down to Rufus. "Is that it?" I said. I stretched my hand out and he rubbed his cheek against it before stalking off into the woods.

I went inside and made a cup of tea.

20

GHOST MAKER

I am a man who creates ghosts for a living. *Ghost Catcher* is in its fourth season now, and I've been there since the beginning as their only cameraman. I'm sure you've seen it on the Paranormal Channel, at least the commercials. Two friends dedicated to unveiling the truth about the supernatural after a shared high school experience. In reality, Jamie and Trent are two pretty faces picked up by the production company to run around in the dark and get excited about "orbs." They're household names now. You can even buy t-shirts with their fake-tan faces on them. I make fun of them, but they're genuine guys. They really believe in this supernatural stuff. They know about the fake stuff we pull, but all the things they say on the talk shows about the show being like a big happy family—they mean it.

Today we're at an old Cape in Connecticut. The owner is typical of who we get writing in: a housewife with a homely face and too-bright lipstick. She has good hair, though, and when I look over at Bob, the production manager, his eyes are big and shiny like a puppy. He has a soft spot for women like her.

"Dave," he says to me, "show the young lady the new camera," and I oblige. I can see Bob's round face going red when she smiles at him. He's been lonely since his wife left him last year. He just wants someone to go home to after work. His ex got bored with him and started going to night classes and retreats. Last I heard, she was traveling in Egypt with a women's group. I should just get him on a dating site. Poor guy is so lonely.

I think about my wife and what she'll be like at that age. In my head, I've already divorced myself from Jackie's future. Divorced myself from *her*, but I don't have the balls to do it in actuality. I won't know her when she gets to be that old. I never saw *us* in the future. When she used to talk about growing old together, I let my thoughts drift away to avoid listening to her and I let myself think that one day I would be sure, I would stay or leave. But I just keep floating on; I'm as non-committal as ever.

The housewife thinks she's psychic (they all do), but these days the word is "sensitive." "I've seen a full-bodied apparition," she says, eyes wide. "A Civil War soldier who walked from here"—she points to a threadbare sofa—"to here." With a flourish, she motions to the door and I move the camera. Next we're going to film the attic section. The golden duo isn't here yet; they just come for the night filming.

People think we just film overnight, but what they don't know is that it takes at least a week to film enough that's usable, even with all our trickery. Perhaps *trickery* is too strong a word for it. It doesn't take much to pause a camera in order to make something appear to move on its own: a chair, a bedspread, a Bible if we're going for the demon thing, or use a piece of fishing line to pull the back of someone's sweater. Doors will close on their own with a swift kick, and a disembodied voice can easily rise from the duct system. This is what I spend my life doing.

I'd like to say there's some art to it, but there really isn't. Most of it we don't need to fake: an old furnace will produce the bangs, dust makes great orbs, a creaky floorboard is a godsend, and warm breath in a cold room can make a convincing, eerie mist. I'm sworn to secrecy, but everyone knows. As long as we spook the viewers and get the ratings, no one cares. I think the viewers know, too. Most people aren't that stupid; they just want to be entertained. Occasionally, we have the odd thing we can't explain, but we couldn't make a show on it.

I follow Bob's butt up the steps to the attic. Once we're there, the air is stuffy like any other, and I've been in quite a few. Old toys and Christmas decorations spill out of soggy cardboard boxes. My throat starts to clog with dust and insulation fibers. This place is about as paranormal as Chuck E. Cheese.

"We sometimes sense a young presence here..." I miss the rest of what the woman is saying. I can see Bob trying his best not to ogle her breasts. They're substantial, and heave with emotion as we interview her. Bob has frosting on his chin from eating doughnuts at breakfast. The lady is still talking. "That's why we keep these toys up here. My children have outgrown them now. I could give them to Goodwill..." I think of Jackie. There will be no toys in our attic.

⟫⟫⟫⟪⟪⟪

It was a month ago and a Saturday, late at night; I was at home in the den, flipping through channels. You'd think I'd get sick of TV through work, but I find it hard to sleep, too used to staying awake all night filming. Jackie came and stood in the doorway. She was wearing her fluffy white bath robe, and her pale yellow hair was floating with static. Behind her was the warm glow from the kitchen light. Her face flickered blue with the screen.

"We need to talk," she said. I felt my stomach plunge with a kind of dread tinged with excitement, like when you're a kid and you know you have to have a tooth pulled. I looked over at her. Her features were indistinct, mushy.

"What's the matter?" I thought she was going to tell me it was over. If she ended it, then I wouldn't have to. I turned the TV sound off. It wasn't like I just woke up one day and realized I didn't love her. I just coasted along with everything, and at some point realized she loved me more than I loved her. She didn't say it was over, however. She walked over to the couch, sat beside me and took my hand.

"We're having a baby."

I looked at her. She squeezed my hand and I looked into her eyes that seemed brown in the dark, even though they're blue. They were open wide and I could see a reflection of the TV screen in each iris. She was doing that smile where she shows all her teeth. When I didn't say anything, her smile got smaller. Her face diminished.

"We're having a baby, David. I'm three weeks along." She raised her hand and picked at the dry skin on her lip. I'd seen her do this many times.

"Have you taken a test?"

Her brow furrowed. "Yes, of course. You were away filming and I couldn't wait."

I sat and looked at her and tried to rearrange my face into something that was appropriate. Her eyes were searching my face and I couldn't quite keep up with them, make it right.

"Aren't you?" she said. I almost looked around to see if she was talking to me.

"You have to get rid of it," I said.

She looked at me in silence. It may have been seconds, it may have been minutes, but time seemed to stretch and slow. I noticed an itch behind my knee. When time sped up again she began to sob, dry, heaving gulps that didn't make a sound. She didn't look away or close her eyes. Her gaze didn't move. I sat there with her limp hand in mine and wished I was somewhere else.

We kill the lights in the Cape as the sun goes down. I film Jamie and Trent as they stalk through the kitchen. Trent holds up an EMF reader and shouts out readings while Jamie explains to the audience: "Some people believe electromagnetic fields are evidence of spirits. Ghosts use this energy to manifest. We could be in the presence of the supernatural." More likely it's the refrigerator kicking out rays, but who am I to say? Next Trent pulls out a digital sound recorder to capture EVPs. We'll review them later and see if we can get the white noise to say "Get Out!" but for now we wander into the hallway, asking questions into thin air. I found a talking doll upstairs that's going to go off on its own, and later we'll walk up and down the stairs for the camera's microphone to pick up. Jamie turns and gives me a wholesome grin; I wish someone would tell him that the infra-red doesn't pick up tan.

Off camera, Bob is talking to the housewife. "Of course we believe that this house is haunted. It's not just for the TV. Spirits don't work on a schedule, I'm afraid, but we do. It's just to help it along. I really hope that we do catch some real activity, and then we won't need all this." He smiles at her crestfallen face. It occurs to me that I don't even know if Bob believes in the paranormal. I know about his failed marriage, his problems with his weight and the fact that he's borderline diabetic, yet I don't know his opinions on the very thing we work together on.

I want to tell him about Jackie, but I know he'll be disappointed in me. I can just imagine the look in his eyes when I tell him that my wife is pregnant and I'm making her get rid of the baby.

We move to the living room. Trent and Jamie try to make contact with the ghost of the soldier. We don't mix it up much on this show. There's a formula we stick to. It's a formula that works, though—for the ratings, rather than finding actual ghosts. Jamie asks: "Is there anyone there? Give us a sign. Show us your presence," and nothing happens. They make a big deal on this show about it being dark, but what they don't mention is that I'm in the dark, too, and walking backwards; I have the torn-up ankles to prove it. What I see is the little square on the viewing screen in front of me as I stumble backwards into the unknown.

We return to the kitchen. We had debated having some plates fly around, but in the end decided to go for the Civil War angle. It's a popular one in New England. Bob begins to go upstairs with his boots on to do the heavy footsteps. We joke about him being the heaviest, and he laughs. I wonder if he ever regrets not having kids. Maybe his wife would have stayed if they had. Once we get the footsteps wrapped up, I go into the attic to check the camera.

After Jackie had finished crying, we went to bed. I stared at the ceiling while she lay with her back to me. We didn't talk. What could we say? I stayed awake for a long time, and it wasn't just the usual insomnia. I could tell by her breathing that she wasn't asleep either. She lay very still. I could hear her gulping and snuffling. I reached out to touch her, but stopped before my hand connected with her skin.

Years ago she had said things like, "When we have kids." That had changed to, "If we have kids," and then it had stopped. I assumed the matter had been dropped, that she was thinking along the same lines as me. I thought about the madness of me being a father, of something swimming around in Jackie that we had made. How could I have created that spark of life without some sort of sign? I wondered if the thing was a person yet, if it had a soul. Where does its soul go if we get rid of it? If Jackie doesn't have this kid, will I be making a ghost?

The next morning, she wouldn't talk to me, wouldn't look at me, but once I'd been away to work and come home again, she thawed. We talked, awkwardly, about nothing important. Later, she showed me the appointment letter. I nodded and told her I'd be away filming.

Despite the mustiness, I like hanging out in attics. Give me an attic rather than a basement any day. The camera is set up fine, so I root around in a few of the boxes, flip through some old magazines, and find a stack of yearbooks where the pictures of bad eighties haircuts are spotted with water damage. Right at the back, I see a lawn chair and wonder if I can balance it across the joists. I walk across the beams and drag it over to where it's not in shot. I figure I have a bit of time to relax before the others get here to film the next section. I turn off the light and settle into the chair. My shoulders are knotted, and I've been clenching my jaw so hard I have a headache. I open my mouth a couple of times to ease the pressure.

I'll call Jackie in the morning. She deserves more than that, but she has her appointment at the clinic tomorrow. I'll tell her I think she should go ahead with the abortion. Tell her that everything is going to be all right. Tell her we'll get through this, even though I don't believe it myself.

The chair is comfy and the attic is hot. I close my eyes, tilting my head back on the head rest. The tension drops from my shoulders; my arms dangle over the sides of the chair. As I start to drift into sleep, all my body hair stands on end. I sit up and look around. It's dark, but I see the outline of boxes in the light filtering from downstairs, where the others are bumping around. It won't be long before they're up here. The air in the attic gets colder, and I wonder where I've left my jacket. I rub my arms with the palms of my hands. For once, I'm desperate for sleep and settle back into the chair. Not very professional, but it's not the first time someone has fallen asleep on this job.

I half-dream about Jackie, the way she sits on the bed and brushes her hair. How the blonde strands rise up to meet the bristles as she moves to the crown of her head. I fall into the rhythm of it, the rise and fall of her arm, the tilt of her head.

It's then I feel a tiny hand rest on my forehead. It wakes me. I know I'm not asleep. I am not dreaming. It is not a breeze and it is not a spider web. It is a child's hand that is so soft and so small that I want to grab hold of it and squeeze it. I feel the fingertips and the palm and the side of the thumb, resting as if checking whether I have a fever. Only two people have ever felt my head like this: my mother when I was very young, and Jackie. I don't move because I don't want to disturb it. I open my eyes wide, but even in the dark I can see there is no one there. The hand feels warm and dry. I think of what the woman said about the presence. I don't want it to go. I can feel it breathing on me. Small, feathery breaths, warm and quick. How the hell can it be breathing? I sit there for two or twenty minutes—I lose track—with the hand placed on my forehead. It never moves and the pressure doesn't change. The breathing on my face gets closer and closer. I think about Jackie and her blue eyes that look brown in the dark. I think about how I'm making her get an abortion. I think about her blonde hair. I tell whatever is there, "Sorry," and the breathing gets really close then. Small, dry lips indent my cheek.

Then the hand is gone. I whisper, "Come back," but I know it is no longer there. I wipe the grit of fiberglass from my eyes and squint into the room. When Bob throws open the attic door, appearing in a square of yellow light, I am still in the dark, exploring my forehead with my fingertips and trying to hide from him that I am crying.

Later, Bob will walk away with the housewife's phone number. Turns out she's divorced and lonely too. Jamie and Trent will finish their close-ups and then swan off in their top-of-the-range RV. I'll walk down those attic stairs on wobbly legs, call Jackie and tell her to stop. Cancel the appointment. If she wants that baby, then she should have it. No matter what my opinion is. As for me and her? I still don't know. I just know that this particular ghost is not mine to make.

But for now, I have to put batteries in this doll. It says, "Mama," and the whole attic space is filled with its electronic voice.

SERMON FROM NEW LONDON

Sistren, I thank you all for gathering here today with me in our holiest of places, the Casbah. Times are hard and you all barely have time for this. There are water and supplies to gather before the season of poison mist hits, but take time for this old woman who may not make it to St. Westwood's Day. I must prepare for the future without me in it. One day soon, one of you will take my place as Superior Poet Patti, and it is my solemn duty to relay to you the history of our founder.

Before that, let us all perform the holy double clap together. Join me in thanks to Anti-Christ, Johnny Rotten, and Our Lady, Joan Jett. Raise your hands, sistren.

Not many of you know that our founder, the Dishonorable Jen of the Fucking Suburbs, was my flesh sister. We were born of the same womb in the time before the storm. Jen was two years older than me, and I confess that we did not always get along. It took a long time before I understood the wisdom in her message. These were the days of the last president, and I am ashamed to say that I was comfortable in my privilege. My life had not changed then. I had no idea of the struggles that would befall all of us.

Jen was an embarrassment to me. Something happened to her when she got to high school. She got her nose pierced and dyed her hair. She only wore ripped jeans, black t-shirts, and Doc Marten boots. She carried around an old ripped blue Navy backpack that she scrawled on in marker: Anarchy signs and *Punk is Not Dead* and *Fuck the President* and bands I'd never heard of then. I burned with shame when she passed my friends and me in the hall. I averted my eyes to avoid contact. My friends would titter as she walked by. She wouldn't look at us. She would hold her head up high as she extended her middle finger in our direction.

At home she would play old LPs: The Clash, The Descendants, The Sex Pistols, Bad Brains, The Stooges, all our sacred texts. Back then, the use of records had fallen out of practice, not like now. This was when the internet still existed; there were Spotify and Pandora, people had downloads. Don't give me your "What is the internet?" I've explained it before. May Siouxie bless us that we never go back to those times. I know it's hard for you to understand, but just remember that my sister Jen, your Jen, knew how to pick out the jams, motherfuckers, just as the prophets foretold.

Did I know then, in the deep kernel of my heart, of the truth that was being revealed to my sister? I did not. She began dating Demetrius, Kind-hearted Demetrius of the Wrong Side of the Tracks. I loved him like a brother. He was kind to me even when I didn't deserve it, when my own sister wouldn't look at me.

Repeat after me: Punk is not dead.

Punk is not dead.

My friends were scared little girls, only acting tough when they perceived there was no danger. "Those people," and they would tilt their heads, "those people, are just not civilized... should go back to where they came from...SHOULD BE GRATEFUL." Where did these girls get this stuff from? Their parents mostly, the radio, the internet, the last president. I thought I could tune them out. I was wrong, sistren. You can't turn your back on hate. Remember the wise words of the inviolable Dead Kennedys and tell all Nazis to fuck off. Because that's what these girls were, my loves: baby fascists in the making.

I am tired. I have seen much. May my lust for this life continue, my sisters. I'll see another Year of our Lord Johnny yet.

I could tell you all kinds of things. How that dead religion preached love for all but its followers only practiced it on the few; how, in the days of the last president, it became clear that you had to take sides and crazy Jen of the Fucking Suburbs was on the right side. But what really swung me, started me on this path that brought me in front of you now, was a fight. A fight amongst school children.

I was walking in the corridor when I felt a tap on my shoulder. It was Demetrius. My so-called friends scattered like marbles. "Your mom's sick," he said. "Nothing serious, but she won't be able to pick you up from the bus stop tonight. You can ride home with Jen and me." I nodded. Then a large white hand appeared on Demetrius's shoulder and swung him around. It was the older brother of one of my friends.

"How dare you talk to her," he said. I looked around and then realized he was talking about me. I began to protest.

"It's okay," I said. "Demetrius was just..."

The brother put his hand up to my face. "Stay out of this. We'll handle it..."

I can see you all smirking. I know it sounds unbelievable, a boy interrupting ME? But it happened, my sistren, and a boiling pit of anger inflamed in my stomach and that fire has never gone out.

"Fuck off, dude," said Demetrius, and that's all it took for them to fall on him. Everything went in slow-motion then: the kicks and the punches, the blood flying. Demetrius could always handle himself, but there were so many of them. I paused, looked behind me, and saw all those girls lined up to spectate. They were the ones who had caused this. I looked upon their ghastly faces and I knew they had not done it to protect me. Time sped up; I looked around and saw Demetrius getting badly hurt, and I knew whose side I was on. I screamed like a Banshee and ran towards them. I jumped on the brother's back and screeched in his ear. I clawed his face. But I was small then, and not capable of much damage. Then I heard Jen's voice herald like a battle cry.

"You motherfuckers!" I saw her then, charging down the corridor, Dishonorable Jen of the Fucking Suburbs, swinging her backpack over her head like a mace. She threw it at one kid's groin, and then with a flying kick of those Doc Martens, she booted the brother in the head. We fought them off, sistren, or at least we held our own until the adults came.

It's okay to cheer, yes, let's have a round of applause for Jen and Demetrius and me.

In fact, sing with me: *Fuck you, we won't do what we're told to!*

Fuck you, we won't do what we're told to!

FUCK YOU, WE WON'T DO WHAT WE'RE TOLD TO!

Is there more to this story? Oh yes, my loves. This is your history, and I must tell you once more before I greet the earth for the final time. Let me go on, sistren, before I am listed in our sun.

ST. SCHOLASTICA'S HOME FOR CHILDREN OF THE SEA

I was barely out of childhood myself when I started working at St. Scholastica's. I didn't have much use for school, not being academically inclined. I'd missed much, being the eldest daughter of a house full of children that I had to help my mother look after. My father was either at the mill or at the drink, so when Mother Gentiana told my mother that she needed help at the orphanage, I was sent within the week. I would be clothed, fed, and my wages sent home. My next sister along could take over my duties.

My mother took me to one side the night before I left. "It'll be strange at the orphanage. You'll see and experience things different to what it's like here in the village," she said.

"I know, Mother. I know that Mother Gentiana keeps things separate. I know I'll be away from you all."

"It's not just that," she said. "Those kids." She paused. "Those kids'll need all your love and attention. They'll be...different. You've heard the tales. But you pay no mind to that, remember we're all children in God's eyes, deserving all the same. I hope I brought you up to remember that."

I reached out and held her hand. "You have, Mother. I hope I'll do you proud."

"I know you will," she said, and kissed my forehead.

The next day, Mother Gentiana herself came to drive me to the orphanage in her battered truck. The Mother was a tall, hawkish woman dressed in overalls and work boots. Her only concession to her station was the traditional wimple and veil she wore to cover her head. We barely spoke during the two-hour drive through the woods and into the hills. She asked me facts: how many brothers and sisters I had, where we worshipped, if at all, where I had gone to school and been born. She offered no information about herself.

St. Scholastica's was an iron-gray, domineering building at the top of a hill hidden by trees. It was high enough that when the wind hit right, you could smell the sea in the air. At first look I assumed it to be stone, but as I stood underneath its looming walls, I could see it was the regular old shingles we all had on our houses, just forgoing the usual New England white. It was different up here. I felt enclosed by the pines and sensed a thousand faces peering at me from the blank windows. Mother Gentiana took a massive iron key out of her pocket to unlock the door and ushered me in, shouldering my heavy bag alone. "Let me show you your room," she said, and I followed her up the narrow staircase.

I didn't mind the orphanage. The work was hard, but no harder than I had to work at home. No schoolwork to bother me, and a luxury I had never dreamed of: my own room. They kept me away from the children at first. I suppose they thought I needed time to adjust, to get used to living away from home, before showing me the true nature of my charges. They needn't have worried. As far as I was concerned, the children were loves. I had a natural aptitude for soothing babes, and they were no different in that respect. Besides, I had an affection for outsiders. Our poverty and my parents' moral disintegration had made us outcasts of a sort in the village, and I had already heard the stories. We all had. In fact, I was eager to see one of the orphanage's residents after I had heard so much about them. My large and strong body was soft and matronly, and my low voice meant for crooning. I found my place there at St. Scholastica's. Others were not so lucky.

I'll never forget the first time I got the smallest glimpse of one of the children. I had been charged with carrying some laundered linens to the top floor of the orphanage, where the smallest babes were. It was a job I often got, being one of the strongest. The top corridor was one of the darkest, with no natural light and lower ceilings than the rest of the house. Gaslights flickered in sconces along the dark walls, barely lighting the way. There was no electricity up here, but I admit that this was my favorite part of the orphanage. There was always quiet up here; you rarely heard any crying.

The darkness and closeness gave a cocoon-like feeling. I stopped at the end door and knocked. I knew I wasn't allowed to go into the rooms yet. I placed the laundry basket on the floor. I was about to leave and walk back down the corridor when I heard a loud thump coming from inside the room. It was the sound of something heavy and wet smacking onto the floor, hard enough that it reverberated through the floorboards under my feet. I then heard a cute little giggle, a baby laugh, and the nursemaid exclaim, "Oh, you little bugger! Fast as bleeding lightning!"

"Is everything okay?" I shouted through the door. I could hear a strange noise, a slithering across the floor and footsteps after it.

"We're fine, love," said the nursemaid, out of breath. "Don't dally. You shouldn't be here."

"Yes, ma'am," I said, and turned to go. There was no way I wanted to get in trouble with Mother Gentiana. Before I left, the door opened slightly and the creak of it caused me to turn back around. A tiny little limb snaked through the crack in the door, a purple limb that had suckers running all along its underside. It reared up and waved at me. There was that little chortle again.

"Oh no, you don't," said the nursemaid, her voice just on the other side of the door. "It's time for your dinner." I heard a grunt as the nursemaid picked up something heavy and the little limb slipped back inside the door.

For the most part, my early days at the orphanage were grunt work. I carried laundry and put wood on the fire, I picked potatoes in the field next door and washed vegetables by the bucket-load. I did not go to the village or visit my family for over a year. I didn't mind. I was built for the work. It was tiring. I worked all day and flopped into my bed after dinner. Mother Gentiana kept me apprised of my family, so I knew there was no cause to worry beyond the usual. I would venture to say I was satisfied rather than happy, but that was to change.

The only dark spot in my days was Lucia. Lucia was another girl who had started working at St. Scholastica's six months before I had. Lucia was spiteful and mean; there was no other way to put it. Tall and red-haired with doughy, freckled arms, the only reason she didn't pick on me outright was because I matched her in size. That didn't mean she couldn't snipe, snipe, snipe at me constantly. She criticized my work, my looks, my voice, my very existence. I never heard a nice word escape from her lips. My only consolation was that she was exactly the same with everyone else. She disliked every single one of us. I wondered if she even liked herself. I worried that she behaved the same way with the children. I overheard one of the nursemaids ask Mother Gentiana why she had brought Lucia to St. Scholastica's. Her reply was vague: "Sometimes a person's situation is so dire that you have a calling to save them, whether they deserve it or not, or are grateful." She could not be coaxed into saying anything further.

It was because of Lucia that I was finally able to see the children, earlier than perhaps Mother Gentiana had intended, and while the circumstances were not the best, especially for Lucia, I cannot deny that being closer to the children made me happier.

Bath day was always a big day at St Scholastica's. It only happened once a month, and usually I was sent downstairs to the kitchen to begin to soak and wash the towels after they had been used. It was hard, slimy work and I did not relish it. It was a relief then when Mother Gentiana asked me to take more soap upstairs to the bathroom. I was to leave it outside the door, as I did with the laundry, and come straight back down.

I had told no one of the little limb I had seen earlier that month. I went up the stairs to the washrooms and placed the soap, as instructed, on the floor outside the door. It was then I heard Lucia screech, her tone as angry and as nasty as usual. "Don't you... Don't you dare!" There was a splash of water on the floor and a giggle. Lucia bellowed. "You little freak! I told you not to!" There was a loud slap. "That'll teach you," she snarled. Then Lucia began to make another noise, a noise I had never heard a human make before, an unearthly noise. The only thing I could compare it to is the sound of a pig screaming when it knows it is going to the slaughter, only much, much worse.

Lucia's screams echoed through St. Scholastica's, and Mother Gentiana and an army of nursemaids came running to her aid. I was pushed aside in the rush. I slammed against the wall and slid to sit on the wooden floor. I stayed put, unable to put together the sounds that I was hearing, squelching and slithering and things breaking, Lucia's cries getting weaker and weaker. The Mother and the maids were too late. When they finally pulled Lucia out of there, there was nothing left of her face; just bloody pulp where her fierce frown had been. Most of her bones were clearly broken, and a rash of livid sucker marks pocked her skin.

That night, I sat on the hearth of the fireplace in the kitchen. The cook had made me some hot milk to help me sleep, but I was unsure that I would ever rest easy again. Lucia's screams echoed in my head and every time I closed my eyes, the image of her broken body swam inside the darkness of my eyelids. Mother Gentiana came in and sat on the rocking chair by the fire. I could see by the way she sank into the cushion and closed her eyes that she was bone-tired and heartsick, but as the cook passed her a mug of milk, she opened her eyes and looked at me.

"Did you ever have a cat at home, Mercy?" It was the first time she had ever called me by my name.

"Yes, Mother," I said. "Tabby, she was my mother's."

"And was Tabby a mouser?" she said.

"Aye, she was quite the huntress. She'd get mice, and birds, voles, and a salamander once."

Mother Gentiana nodded. "Did she eat her kills?"

"No, she left them as presents, usually for my mother. Sometimes they weren't quite dead. My mother said she was contributing to the household."

Mother Gentiana gave me a weary smile. "Your mother was right. It's a sad thing, though, to see the little broken bodies, yes?"

I nodded. "Mother always wanted me to throw them in the woods, but I couldn't. I gave them a proper burial."

"You didn't blame the cat, though? It was just following nature."

I nodded. "It's what they do."

"Cats," she said, "and especially kittens, are cute little things, but they are predators. They murder by instinct. The same goes for the children here, Mercy. It's in their nature, their being. It's part of their survival instinct. Lucia hurt them, threatened them, so they reacted on instinct. Are you scared of cats, Mercy?"

"No."

"You have no reason to be scared of the children either. They are babes still, innocents. When they grow older, they will go to the sea, where they will have to kill to survive. But that is in the future. Right now they are in our care and it is our duty to look after them. Do you understand?"

"Yes, Mother Gentiana."

The Mother rose from her chair, the wood creaking, and reached her hand out to me. "Come on, it's time you met the children."

I took her hand and followed her to the dormitories. As we walked up the creaking stairs, she said, "The children are still quite upset about today's incident, so we have put them all in the same dormitory. They tend to feel safer together."

"Where's Lucia?" I said.

"We buried her in the woods. If anyone asks, she ran away with a boyfriend and we don't know where she is."

I wonder: if it had been anyone other than the hated Lucia, would I have cared more? I don't think so. Even then, before I had met them, my sympathies were with the children. I would never be able to explain it, but I suspect Mother Gentiana knew. Otherwise, she would have said more, tried to convince me to keep quiet. She knew I wouldn't tell and we never spoke of the lie again, although Lucia was, of course, all tied up in what came after.

The dormitory was warm and smelled of babies, newborns, that distinctive smell when you put your face to the still-forming crown of their head. It is an intoxicating smell, and the air was full of it. It took a while for my eyes to adjust to the dim light of the gas lamps, but when they did, I could see the room was full. There were tiny beds and cots and bassinettes everywhere, the room a sea of worn linen and children.

The children were all different sizes, from newborns in the nursemaids' arms to older babies, toddlers, right up to little girls and boys around five years old. All of them had something that made them not quite human, something that bound them to the sea. Many of them had octopus limbs instead of legs; others had tentacles instead of arms, many had beaks, others again had appendages on the lower portions of their faces. At least one had a mouthful of shark teeth, and another the light of an anglerfish, and yet they were all human enough for me to recognize how young they were, big blue and brown eyes, tiny hands and downy hair. Those that could smile at me did, with baby teeth missing or not grown in yet. Mother Gentiana pushed me ahead.

"Go on then, say hello." I walked among them, touched their little hands and stroked their heads, waved at the shy ones and told them my name. One of the nursemaids handed me a baby, and I knew it was the one I had seen that day. He wrapped one of his little purple limbs around my wrist and laid his head against my chest as he sucked his thumb. They called him John. How to explain how I felt at that moment? Lucia was forgotten, and I knew that I would do anything in my power to protect and care for these children.

After that, St. Scholastica's truly became my home and happiness. I was Mother Gentiana's protégé. She showed me all of the workings of the orphanage, from the kitchens to the laundry to the garden and the grounds. She had originally been from the village, like me, whereas the cook and the stable boy had come from other parts of Maine. The nursemaids came from over the sea, Ireland and the north of England mostly. I asked her whether I should take vows, and she said no. "I took mine before we knew of this." She swung her arm towards the orphanage. "It's clear that there is more to this world than what is in that dusty book, but don't tell anyone I said that." She winked at me. "What matters is what's in your heart."

What was is my heart was those children. It was as if I had been cracked open at the core, and they were the light that was let in. In addition to my practical chores of making sure they were fed, clean and rested, I played with them and cuddled them, rocked them when they were sleepy and wiped away their tears when they were hurt. My especial favorite was John. He would slide over to me as soon as I entered the room and pull at my skirts to be picked up. I spent many a day doing my work with him at my hip. I didn't mind, I never minded. I tried not to think of the day when they would leave for the sea.

"There'll be other children," said Mother Gentiana. "There's always more."

When it was clear I was going to stay, Mother Gentiana allowed me to come down to the village to get supplies and visit my family. My stay with my folks was brief. "You've changed, girl," slurred my father as he walked out the door, the smell of grain alcohol following him. I could see that he hadn't. My mother was pleased to see me, and I was heartened to witness my sisters and brothers growing up more responsible than my parents, frankly. As I made my way to leave, my mother caught my arm.

"I can see by how well and happy you look that I did the right thing sending you up there," she said. "I stand by what I said before you left. But be careful, things are changing here. Not everyone thinks of that place and the poor souls in it like I do, and there's been talk in the village since that girl disappeared. Her folks have been stirring up some bad feelings. I worry for you all." I patted her arm and kissed her cheek and told her I would, but I wasn't worried. Surely everyone knew that Lucia was trouble. I would have been surprised if her parents were any better or taken seriously. I'd lived in the village all my life. I knew most were good people at heart.

Later that day, I was at the store with the Mother. I could feel someone's stare boring into my back and as I turned to go, a weak-looking man with strawberry blond hair and dark circles under his eyes spat on the floor in front of us. Mother Gentiana ushered me out. When we got to the truck, I asked her who it was.

"Lucia's father. Best to stay away from him."

When I returned to the orphanage, there was a letter from my brother:

Mam doesn't know this, but the rest of us think you should come back home. There's been a lot of talk in the village. Lucia's dad, he's been very loud. He's got some big shots from Boston backing him up. They're saying that it is unnatural for those...things to exist. They're saying we shouldn't be looking after them. They're monsters, Mercy. They should be exterminated. Come back. We, your brothers, can protect you then. If you don't, then you're one of the monsters too.

I dismissed the letter. I was angry at my brother for patronizing me and got back to work.

A month or two went by, but then the stable boy showed up from a trip to the village battered and beaten, clutching a ripped poster in his hands. He showed it to Mother Gentiana as we hustled to get warm soapy water to clean the cuts on his arms and face. "The boys from the village got me when I ripped it down," he said. "They said that they were going to tell the men. That I would be sorry. Mother, I'm sorry to bring this on you, on us all. I just couldn't stand to see them call the children monsters."

Mother Gentiana gave a heavy sigh. "It's not your fault. It was only a matter of time. They were looking for an excuse."

"What's going on?" I said.

"There are certain...groups," she said, "factions, who disagree with our work. They dress it as faith, but it's not. It's money and politics and havoc to them." She handed me the poster. There was a cartoon monster on it, devouring human children.

Join us for a village supper, it said. *We're here to help you with your monster problem. Tired of sharing your home with dark beasts? Find a sympathetic ear with us. Join us. We will fight for you. We will fight for your children. We will protect your interests. We are of the Faith.*

Mother Gentiana sighed again. "I wonder how they found us. They usually turn up in larger towns and cities."

"Lucia's father," said the stable boy, "went all the way to Boston to get them. Her mother told me." He nodded his head towards me. "Though she said she couldn't be seen talking to me. Feelings were running high, she said."

"They won't do anything to us," I said. "The village. The orphanage has always been here. No one's ever minded."

"People change their minds," said Mother Gentiana. She walked to the closet under the stairs, where we kept coats and overshoes. After rustling in the back, she pulled out a shotgun. "Bed the animals down," she said to the stable boy, "then come back here and make sure we're all locked up. We have to be ready, just in case."

I would like to say that nothing came of it. I would like to say that my assessment of the village, of the people I had known all my life, was correct. But I was wrong, and just after the meeting must have ended, they arrived in their trucks and cars. Flaming torches, just like the angry villagers of old stories, ready to take on the monsters. I didn't recognize all of them—perhaps they were men from out of town who made up most of the mob—but the rest, I did. I was endlessly relieved that none of my kin were there, but there was Lucia's father, at the fore, his face twisted in hate.

"If you only knew what that man had done to his own daughter whom he professes to miss so much," said the Mother. "Take the children upstairs," she said to the nursemaids. We waited for the hammering on the door. It wasn't long. The door splintered like firewood and they surged into the room like a dangerous tide. The stable boy tried to fight, but he was already injured. It took a couple of men mere seconds to overwhelm him. Mother Gentiana managed to shoot one before being knocked over, her head ringing on the stone hearth. She didn't move, her skin the color of mushrooms, so I grabbed the gun and ran up the stairs after the men, the cook screaming behind me.

How did they know where the children would be? A lucky guess? A traitor in our midst? We would never know, but they headed straight to the dorm where all the babes were. They crashed through the door even more easily than they had the first. Some were not as brave as they supposed themselves to be, taking flight as soon as they saw our children, running down the stairs like frightened rabbits. Others' disgust soon transformed to murderous hate. Lucia's father made a grab for John and I shot the man dead. I confess no remorse for this murder. John reached out to me, and I grabbed him and held him close. Of course, this focused the men's attention on me, and they came at me, throwing the brave nursemaids who tackled them out of the way.

Then there was a change in the air. A high-pitched hum came from deep in John's throat. All of the children responded to it and joined in the noise. The sound got louder and louder, filling the room. It was all the sign they needed. It was as when they retaliated on Lucia, except much, much more. They moved fast, faster than I had ever seen them move, and they were on the men before the men knew what hit them.

The weapons the men had, pistols, knives and torches, were useless at such speed. By the time they tried to draw them, limbs and tentacles had torn them out of their hands. It was then the real massacre happened, quickly, a frenzy. The children used their monstrous tools to tear those men apart, limb from limb. Blood was a mist that filled the room. A fine spray covered the linens. Deadly suckers held on fast as they dislocated joints and broke bones; those with beaks and those with teeth rended flesh and tendon. In no time at all there was little left of the men who had invaded our home.

When they were done, they all gathered behind me, hiding behind my skirts like the children they were. "It's okay," I soothed. "You had to protect us. You did what is in you to do. Remember this when you go to the seas." I turned to the nursemaids. "If any of you want to go, go now, but you can never come back." They all stayed still. I stumbled down the stairs still carrying John. Mother Gentiana was alive. Insensible, but breathing.

I found one of the men from the group cowering in the kitchen.

"Your friends are dead," I said. "Go to the village. Tell them the men are gone. Tell them that it is my duty to look after these children and that we will continue to do so. Tell them not to try this again." I pushed him out the doorway. "What are you looking at?" I asked those assembled. "The Mother needs help and we have an orphanage to run. It's way past the children's bedtime."

I smiled at John. I wiped a smear of blood from his tiny cheek. He smiled back at me. I was home indeed.

CRAB

"Audrey, I'm going to see what he's up to." Jim looked down at his wife. Nose buried in a book as she spread her legs out to tan, she didn't acknowledge his existence. Jim hated the beach. He hated the sun and the suntan cream and the sand; they all seemed to conspire to make him uncomfortable, hot, sticky and itchy. It didn't help that Audrey adored the seaside. He looked at her blotchy legs, greasy with lotion, the small pale brown freckles on her knees that he used to find endearing. The red skin on her thighs looked tight and ready to burst like overcooked sausages. One of those true crime books she always seemed to be reading lay on her lap and as his gaze traveled up her torso he was confronted by her cleavage, her massive breasts barely restrained by flowered spandex. On her head was a ridiculous, floppy sunhat, a relic from the seventies, just like the two of them.

"You're in my sun, Jim," she said.

Jim went to sit back down again, thought better of it, and straightened back up. He looked down the beach. His nine-year-old son was keeping himself busy with something near the water's edge. Jim lumbered over to James, named after him, his feet toiling against the dry sand, burning his soles. His son was crouched over something on the sand. Jim stood at a distance at first, watching as James waggled a stick in his hand. Even from behind, the boy had that look of concentration; it bothered Jim to see him so still. It never indicated anything good, in Jim's opinion. His son's hunched back looked small, his body thin and pale, looking blue in parts, his skin almost translucent, ribs poking out like a baby bird's. He looked younger than he was.

"What you up to, James?" Jim was aware of the fake cheerful quality that affected his voice every time he tried to have a reasonable conversation with his son. It sounded squeaky, his throat tightening as if it was swelling in the heat. He coughed to try and deepen his tone. Usually, Jim was proud of his voice. It was deep and resonant, if he did say so himself. He'd read something about stress tightening your vocal cords, making you screech. Perhaps that's what was happening? He needed to relax. Why would interacting with his son make him so anxious? He asked again. "What're you doing there, James?"

"Nothing." James didn't turn around. His voice was high, even for a kid. Maybe he was nervous too. Some specific quality in the timbre of James's voice irritated Jim for no reason he could pinpoint.

"Doesn't look like nothing." James didn't answer so Jim walked closer. "What have you got there?"

It was the smell that hit Jim first: the smell of decay and salt and the sea, roadkill smell, almost skunk but not quite. Before James, like a tribute, was the corpse of a horseshoe crab, half hollowed out and rotting. James grinned to himself and dropped his stick. He didn't seem to notice the smell. The corpse was about a foot and a half long to the end of its tail spike, and its body was the size of a small skillet. It was bulbous, shiny, a mosaic of military green and brown. The sand on it looked like frosting. Jim watched, horrified, as James bent down and picked it up, turning it over in his hands, the spindly legs moving like articulated puppet fingers. James didn't look up at his father; he continued to run his fingers over the shell, then held a leg between his thumb and finger, working the joints. Dropping the leg, he picked up the next, worked its joints back and forth, repeated the action over and over, methodically, mechanically.

Jim opened his mouth to say something, to tell James to drop it like you would a dog that's got something in its mouth it shouldn't have, but no noise came out. His mouth flapped open and shut, open and shut, open and shut, the remains of the hot dog he had eaten earlier crawling its way back up his throat. He gagged, choking on it, acid burning his gullet.

James looked up at him, squinting in the sun, and held the horseshoe crab corpse up to him, like he was presenting a prize. Jim could have sworn—no, it must have been the sun, heatstroke—but he could have sworn that the crab began to move of its own volition. Impossible. He took a few steps back, vomited in the sand and looked at it again. That thing was moving. It was moving in James's hands and Jim's nostrils were filled with the stink of its death rot and this could not be happening. Did he have food poisoning? Was he hallucinating? He heard the dry click of those legs moving on their own. Jim looked at his son. There was something sly in that little bastard's face. Jim shuddered and ran up the beach to Audrey, stumbling desperately in the burning sand.

BLACK SHUCK TAVERN

I'm being followed by a huge fucking dog of potentially supernatural origin.

Somewhat ironically, I've been the coat check girl at the Black Shuck Tavern for three years. It was supposed to be a summer job, while I was in college, but...I didn't get very far in college. I was unprepared, and I worried constantly about money. I couldn't shake the feeling that I didn't belong. People from my background don't go to college. I can see now that I was self-sabotaging, but I haven't got together the nerve yet to give it another shot. The Shuck made me feel like I belonged somewhere.

On the strip but set back from the road, the Black Shuck Tavern is understated in daylight hours, a painted matte black cube of a building, but at night the neon sign is switched on—a huge shaggy dog's head, outlined in glowing green, its massive jaws biting down on a cocktail glass. It's the best-looking place on the block. No one walks by it without looking up. Once you get past the bouncers, the doors swing open to a treacherously dim staircase that takes you to the bowels of the building. This is my domain. You can check in your coat or bag or whatever and make your way to the bar or concert room. Everything is painted the same matte black, neon green arrows showing the way, the bar an oasis of light.

The general manager, Felicity, holds court at the end of the bar every night. Felicity is a beautiful blonde trans woman in her 50s who's six-seven in heels. She's been more of a mother to me these past couple of years than my own mother ever was. As I stand at the door, I can tell by the way Felicity is tilting her head that she's making fun of the new bartender, Josh. Josh is a well-spoken, fresh, awkward young man from the East Coast evading going to grad school. Unlike me, Josh has a well-heeled, well-meaning family that he is also evading. He's been here nearly six months. I think we might be starting to have a thing, but I can't quite get my head around it just yet. I duck into the cloakroom, hoping they haven't seen me. "I love you, honey," shouts Felicity. She doesn't miss a thing.

It's not that I don't have offers. I get them all the time. Freshly scrubbed boys in button-down plaid shirts from the Midwest, Canada, Europe. They're here on vacation. The Shuck always attracts a certain kind of crowd, a crowd that's looking for a little bit of danger, a slight tinge of Hollywood's seedy underbelly but the kind that is relatively safe, not the further-down-the-strip, crack house-seedy kind. I guess I fit the bill. I'm a real-life L.A. woman with tattoos and piercings and no visible track marks. They ask me out a lot. It's not my scene. They're not my type, and I'm really not into being the girl you take back to your motel for an away-from-home one-night stand. Give me a fucking break.

So this thing with Josh is throwing me for a loop. He is, ostensibly, just like them, with his neat hair and toothy smile, but at the same time he is not. He seems to be sticking around. He sees past the eyeliner and black clothes. He sees me as a person and not an item on some bullshit "sow your wild oats" checklist. But still, what exactly would I do with a boy like that? We all know that once he's got his rebellion out of his system, he'll go back east to grad school and have a perfect preppy life, and what happens to me then? I've had enough people leave and I don't need any help feeling like I'm not good enough.

I hear shouting from the room behind the cloakroom. The other side is the V.I.P. lounge, and it must be Lawrence trying to get attention. Felicity hustles by me to placate him. She's back after a minute. "Be a doll and go and get Lawrence a bottle of whisky from the bar." She winks at me. We both know that she's fully capable of getting him a drink. She just wants to put me in Josh's general vicinity. She has romantic notions. I mock-sigh dramatically and pull up the counter so I can exit the cloakroom. It's early in the night, and honestly, this is California. Not many people are wearing jackets.

Our interaction at the bar is stilted. Josh *is* good-looking. There's a naivety about him that I find appealing, despite myself. "Can I walk you to your car?" he says. I nod yes. It'll make Felicity happy, if nothing else. Of course, there's the other reason I want him around—I'm being followed by the huge fucking dog, as I mentioned earlier. I can hold my own, but safety in numbers and all that. I ask for the bottle and he passes it over. Everyone knows what type of whisky Lawrence likes. Josh holds the bottle just a beat too long to be comfortable. He's goofy and awkward, and I kind of like that.

Lawrence is the bar owner. When I walk into the V.I.P. lounge, he's slumped over the table looking rough. I'd call him a functioning alcoholic but, well, he doesn't function much. Felicity is an angel, and she keeps this place running. Lawrence props his face up with one hand, and looks at me through one bleary eye, the other closed painfully. He reaches out with his other hand for the bottle. Man, he is ravaged now but still handsome. If you'd have seen him 20 years ago when he bought this place—he was beautiful: rangy and lean, with glossy dark hair and cheekbones for miles. Back in the 90s, Lawrence was the drummer for a grunge band, the only English member from a group from Seattle. He still has the accent. The band made a respectable amount of money. In his more candid moments, Lawrence will admit that they rode on Nirvana's coattails. What he will never admit is that his looks helped a lot. It's almost like he hates that part of himself. He drinks to obliterate his own beauty. He's not the only addict I know. My dad drinks too much ever since Mom left, but she's been gone over a decade, so he long since lost his excuse. We share an apartment on the wrong side of East Hollywood. We keep different hours. I love him but I barely see him. Mom loved smack more than me or Dad. So there you go. I have no idea if she's alive.

Lawrence opens the bottle and takes a long, deep swallow. "You seen the dog recently, girl?" he says. I'm starting to wish I hadn't told him about it.

"Yeah, last weekend."

He pats the padded bench next to him. "Tell me about it. Felicity can handle the club." I go and sit down. He's my boss, what else can I do?

⋙⋘

I've been seeing the dog much longer than Lawrence knows. I used to see it when I was a kid. I know this is true, but I also know that it can't be true. The dog would be much older now, and we didn't even live in Hollywood then. It's so distinctive. I don't know what breed it is, but it's huge and black. Fur so black it looks like the absence of color. Short-haired. I want to say it's a mastiff-type dog, but even that's not right. Its back comes higher than my waist, and I'm a tall woman, and it has this massive blocky head. Its muzzle is wrinkly, velvety and soft, but nearly always curled up into a snarl. What's weirdest about it is its eyes. They're green and big. How many black dogs do you know with green eyes? How do I know that it's not a regular-ass (if very large) dog? I don't, exactly. It's just a feeling, and I'll never be able to explain it.

I know I used to ask my mother if the dog could come in and stay the night. I would be looking out the window, standing on tiptoes to peek over the sill. The dog would be sitting in the street. Dad was out working; he was a truck driver then. Mom would be nodding out on the sofa. She never answered me or came over, so I have no idea if I was seeing a real dog or not. What I do know is that living with a heroin addict as your main grown-up makes a big snarling dog seem not so scary.

I remember seeing it in the parking lot of the hospital when Mom overdosed; as they wheeled her from the ambulance to the doors, I saw it pacing up and down. A lady bustled me into the emergency room before I could go over to it, and when I looked out the window from my mom's room, it was gone.

The last time I saw it as a kid was when my mom left. Dad and I were packing up his truck with our things (Mom had disappeared and Dad had lost his job, so we had to move) and when we set off I saw the dog running behind us on the sidewalk. We hit the highway and I forgot all about it. Until now.

It started again a couple of months ago. It was early hours Saturday morning after closing Friday night. Josh had offered to walk me to my car. I'd turned him down. I barely knew him and hated the insinuation that I couldn't look after myself, even though I knew he was just being nice. "Give me three rings," shouted Felicity as I walked out the door. I always called her when I got into my car and let it ring three times before hanging up, so she knew I got there. I walked downhill off the main strip and took a right down the street I was parked on. About 100 yards before I got to my car, I saw a massive dark shadow cross my path in the light from the street lamps. I knew what it was. It was familiar to me, and that still makes no sense. My heart pounding, I caught a glimpse of its massive black haunch as it slipped between parked cars across the street. I didn't wait to see more. I guess I wasn't as brave as when I was a kid. I knew now what kind of damage a pair of jaws that size could do. Panicking, I ran to my car and got the hell out of there. Felicity called me all mad and teary when I got home.

So I told Lawrence about it, thinking he would get a kick out of it, with the name of the club and everything. I was just making small talk. He freaked out. "Jesus Christ." He lit a cigarette. "It's finally coming for me." I frowned at him, but didn't mention I might have seen it before. He seemed angry, and I wasn't 100% sure he wasn't angry at me. "It's him. It's the Black Shuck. I never should have called this damn place after him. I'm such a cocky shite, thinking I'd escaped him." When I looked nonplussed, he beckoned me to sit. It was midafternoon before my shift. Lawrence was already fall-over drunk. "Back where I'm from, everyone knows about Black Shuck. Some think of him as a legend, others as a ghost, but I'm from a godforsaken backwater where the folks know he's real. He's a big bastard, black like a panther but very obviously a dog. He always shows up when you or someone close to you is about to pop their clogs."

"Pop their clogs?"

"Die, be deceased, kick the bucket." He started cackling. "I dodged him once, then skedaddled over here. They say live fast, die young, but I've hung on probably longer than I've any right to. I was supposed to go then. Drank too much of this." He held up a bottle of whisky. "Even for me. Collapsed outside a pub somewhere in Camden. Just as I was blacking out, he came right over to me and sniffed my face. I wasn't scared. I couldn't move anyway. But I'll never forget his red eyes above me." I started to tell him that I was sure that this dog had green eyes, but he had already passed out. I left him with his head on the table, mumbling about the Black Shuck.

The next time I saw the dog, I'd finally relented and let Josh walk me to my car. He'd asked me a couple of times, and I had always said no, but I admit I was softening, and Felicity overheard once and gave me a pep talk. "Give him a chance," she said. "I hate you walking to your car alone, no matter how tough you think you are."

We were standing at my car, awkwardly. He wanted more, but I was in no way ready to give it to him. At least, I think that was it. He just stood there and stared at me. I said goodnight and was turning to my car door when I saw the Shuck run behind him, darting up the road. I could hear its claws clicking on the pavement. "Did you see that?" I said to Josh.

"What?" he said. I dropped the matter. Gave Felicity three rings and went home.

The last time I saw the dog was last weekend. I leave out the part about finally kissing Josh when I tell Lawrence about it. It's none of his business and honestly, I'm still a bit embarrassed. Josh and I were standing by my car making small talk again, and I'll admit it, he looked cute and I thought... "Why the hell not?" So when he leaned in, I didn't stop him. As we kissed, he bit my lip, probably by accident but hard. It made me jump. As I opened my eyes, I saw the dog sitting behind him on the sidewalk. Black Shuck was sitting like it was waiting for a gigantic treat, like you could pat its humongous head. This time it didn't run. The dog just looked at me with big green eyes. I'd stopped kissing. "Are you okay?" said Josh, and I looked at him for just a second to nod, yes, and when I looked over his shoulder again the dog had gone.

I want to ask Lawrence if he thinks the dog is coming for me, if I'm going to die, but I don't quite believe it. Surely I would be dead by now. I've considered calling the authorities, but who the hell would I call? The police, animal control, Ghostbusters? I think about enlisting Lawrence to call someone, but I immediately dismiss it. An old, drunk, ex-rock star and a hat check girl? What a couple of cranks. I could tell Felicity, but she already worries too much. I don't consider Josh. I don't trust him enough and I don't know why. Besides, I've seen the dog before and I'm still here, so what does it want? Lawrence absolutely thinks it's coming for him. His face gains a deathly pallor and his eyes grow wild every time we talk about it. I don't know why he keeps bringing it up. It's like he's poking his own open wound. He might be right. He's drinking himself to death. He doesn't need the dog to die. I resolve not to mention it if I see it again, even if I have to lie.

I go back to the bar before I settle in at the coat check desk for the night and ask Felicity to go and look in on Lawrence. She'll know what to do. Josh gives me a crooked smile. I think he's trying for sympathetic. I tell him I'll see him later.

The night is long. We're busy, and I think Lawrence is having a rough night. I hear bottles being thrown and glass breaking. Felicity keeps running past me, looking harassed. Josh and I handle the club. Many of the people who come here want to see Lawrence. They get upset when they hear their idol isn't around. It's even more difficult when they can hear him screaming and swearing from the other side of the wall. At the end of the night, Felicity helps Lawrence up to bed. They have adjacent studio apartments above the club. Josh and I lock up and walk to my car.

We don't talk as we walk. We're both exhausted. Our hands brush together, but we don't hold on. I'm unnerved by Lawrence, and I'm worried that I might have started it. It's not like he hasn't had drunken tantrums before, but I feel complicit in this one. Poor Felicity, cleaning up a mess I started. For the first time, I wonder if she's in love with him. No one is that much of a saint. She could get a job in any bar on the strip—she's just that good at her job. It also occurs to me that I don't know where Josh lives. I know he walks to wherever it is, but I don't know if he shares a place with anyone or not. I can't invite him back to mine. How is it that I don't know more about him?

We stand at my car, as awkward as ever. I'm looking around for the dog. Josh asks me if I'm all right. I go in to kiss him, but something's wrong. When I look into his eyes, it looks like it's someone else behind them. He rolls his head, making his neck crack, and I notice that he's built a lot bigger than I ever gave him credit for. His posture has totally transformed: squarer at the shoulders, and his head cocked to one side. He sighs, and says, "I'm getting tired of this, Lacey." His voice sounds different: there's an edge to it, and his accent has changed. He sounds rougher and southern. "I've been very patient." And just like that he grabs me by the throat and slams me against the car. The edges of my vision get dark, but my survival instincts are strong. I'm pummeling him with my fists and kicking at him even as I feel like I'm going to black out. He slams his knee hard into my stomach and it knocks the wind out of me. I try to look up and down the street. No one. Fuck. I'm scratching at his face, but he's like a machine. Who is this guy and why didn't I see this coming?

And then he lets go. He's thrown backwards away from me, flying through the air like he's in a kung fu movie. It's the dog. It's Black Shuck. It shakes Josh around as if he's a chew toy and then pins him on his back on the sidewalk, two huge paws on his shoulders. Those massive jaws snap at his face, and in seconds it's a bloody mess. Before long he's not going to be recognizably human. I snap to my senses, jump in the car and drive, tires squealing down the strip.

I think about calling the police, but fuck Josh, and how could I explain? I doubt there'll be much left of him for anyone to find. Black Shuck did me a favor. I sleep badly but I don't remember my dreams.

⫸⫷

I go to the club early. I apologize to Felicity for not giving her three rings. She's so upset with me, she can barely look at me. Both she and Lawrence are sitting at the bar. I notice they're holding hands. Lawrence has a bit of color in his cheeks for once. "Where's your boy?" he says. I shrug. "We had the coppers here this morning. Seems Josh wasn't exactly telling the truth about himself. You haven't seen him?"

"No," I say. Lawrence notices my bruised neck, touches it gently. Felicity finally looks at me and frowns. She reaches out her other hand to me. I take it.

"Why don't you take the night off?" she says. "Maybe visit with your dad."

"You really don't know where that kid is?" says Lawrence. I shake my head.

"Maybe Shuck got him," I say.

Lawrence grins at me. "You know what else Shuck does? He protects women on their way home."

"She," I say. "My Shuck is a she."

THE LAST WITCH IN FLORIDA

Thanks for interviewing me for your magazine. This is really something. Old women like me are ignored by the media for the most part. I'm the last one? Excellent—I mean, what a shame. Where are they all now? Modern witch hunts up north? Really? Terrible. My name? Meg. I know, pretty stereotypical. I'm 78 years old and I live in Florida. Originally from Salem. No, not that Salem. Salem, Massachusetts. Interesting facts about me? Well... When I've hexed someone, I usually leave a pink flamingo lawn ornament in their yard. Of course, that was a lot more effective when I didn't live in Florida, but I like the ambiguity of it now that I'm here. Those who don't have one usually think it's their tacky neighbor across the street making a joke. Those who have one, same, or maybe they think their partner gifted them one. Some have so many that I'm sure they don't even notice an extra one. I like to do it, though, it's my brand. I buy them in bulk from a warehouse down the road. I keep them in a storage unit I rent.

I've been living at the Sunset Hotel for a couple of years now. Sure, it's seen better days, but I'm fond of it. It's cozy and clean for the most part, and there's a strip mall right across the road with a CVS, my favorite, so it's convenient. I buy boric acid from there and line it up on my windowsills—it keeps the ants away. I used to have a hovel in the woods, cauldron over an open fire, kitchen garden, the whole deal, but I have allergies and I was finding the cold was sinking into my old bones. It took a while to get used to the incessant sunshine, but I'm glad I made the move. I keep occupied.

There's not many of us who are permanent residents at the Sunset, so there's not much camaraderie as such. We'll say good morning, but that's it. There's Paul, who I think is an alcoholic, or perhaps in training to be. He came down here after his divorce. I heard him talking to the desk guy. He stays by the pool, drinking and humming that "Margaritaville" song. There's Dana, who's a single mom with two little ones. Those kids are my exception to the rule. I actually like them. They're timid and meek and don't say much. They hide behind their mother's skirts when they see me—as it should be. Then there's Ginny and Jeff, who I'm fairly sure are cooking meth in their room. The hotel staff are in on it, they've all got quite the racket going on, and who can blame them? They don't get paid enough working at the desk for all hours or cleaning the rooms. Everyone has to do what they can to get by. Ginny and Jeff live at the other side of the hotel, so when their lab inevitable blows up, I think I'll be safe. Live and let live is my motto for the most part, aside from the hexing, of course.

What do I do for fun? Send alligators after people, mostly. That has to be one of the upsides of living in Florida, that and the orchids and the warmth and the waterparks. Sometimes we have guests at the hotel who displease me, shall we say. Noisy groups of bachelors and bachelorettes, obnoxious families who let their little brats run riot: these are the people I set alligators on. A quick ritual with some ingredients from CVS and I can draw them in. From there I send them over to chase the terrible guests, scare them a little. They're literally always hanging around the pool, so it looks perfectly natural. Of course, alligators would be attracted to the water and food. No witchcraft detected. Nobody gets hurt, usually. Depends how fast they can get out of the way. I always make sure the alligators can escape unscathed. It's not their fault people are terrible.

I get most of my clients from the internet these days. It's really revolutionized my business. I have my own website, but you can find me on most social media: Facebook, Twitter. Instagram is especially great for witches. Folks used to have to come and beat a path to my door when I lived in the hovel, ask me for hexes, blessings, spells, all of the above. I know a lot of people my age don't like all the newfangled technology, but I have to say it suits me better. I don't like to interact with humans unless I really have to, and witching online really gives me the freedom to live away from the hovel and do my own thing.

People really do just want hexes these days. They hate each other. Politics, usually. I have my own thoughts on those matters—you can guess, but I don't let it get in the way of business. A buck is a buck and my Social Security gets me nowhere. Until we tear capitalism down, it is what it is: free market hexing! I'd cackle, but I've had a sore throat these last couple of days. I can't remember the last time someone asked for a blessing, or even a love potion, although goddess knows they're not exactly benevolent as a rule. Why? Well, you're making a slave, basically. People want to be loved for themselves these days. It's harder to accomplish, but better, I think.

What are some of my hexes? You want me to give away trade secrets? Well, let's just say I can make folks very, very uncomfortable. I have a sliding scale, depending on the rates—anything from hives to the ultimate: death. I used to get creative with it, but not anymore. I'm old, tired. I do what it says on the tin, nothing more, nothing less. There's so few of us around now, my work is in demand. I wouldn't have it any other way though. I love being a witch.

Ouch! What are you doing with that pin? Get away from me, young man.

No, it's fine. It was just a weird thing to do, is all.

Do I have a familiar? Not anymore, I'm afraid. I had my old cat, Beelzebub, for many years; she died of old age, poor thing, but how I loved her. The Sunset doesn't allow animals in our rooms, so I'm familiar-less for now. Like I said, I do love the alligators, and there are so many great pet videos on social media these days. The cats are my favorite, then raccoons, I think.

Can I put a spell on you? Of course, but for a fee. I don't work for free. What's that the kids say? Pay the artist? Well, pay the witch, too. It *is* an art, you know, an art and a craft and I've been practicing for years. I do the best spells. What is it you would like? Have a think about it, we can sort out the terms after the interview.

I haven't had a coven in years. I don't do well with people, like I said. I'm a loner at heart. You know all the problems you get working in an office? Same with covens. That's why I keep to myself. I tried a couple of times. Joined some groups. I just never felt like I fit in. How much of a misfit do you have to be to not fit in to a coven? I wonder where they all are now. If they're really all gone.

I like swimming, actually. That was one of the main things I wanted when I moved down here: somewhere to sit in the sun, and a nice pool. For a hotel of this...caliber, shall we say, the pool area is really nice and they keep it very clean, not like some of the other places I looked at before I settled in here. Have you any idea how many hotels are just fine with turds floating in their pools? Human turds, too! I'd blame it on the kids again, but I think it's just as likely that the old folks like me are responsible. No, I don't want to swim now. I haven't even got my bathing suit on. Stop nudging me. You're a strange young man.

Nipples! How dare you? What a question to ask an old lady. I have the regular amount, I'll have you know, and even if I didn't, what business is it of yours?

Look, let's cut to the chase, young man. You and I both know that you're no journalist. Do you think I'd have lasted this long in the woods, or Florida, for hell's sake, if I was as gullible as you seem to think I am? I knew you were a witchfinder as soon as you sent me that DM on Twitter, never mind your clumsy line of questioning. I could smell it on you before you turned into the parking lot. Do you think I got to be the last of my kind without offing a witchfinder or two, or twenty? Hear that? That's the cackle of a real witch. I don't have a sore throat. What kind of witch can't cure a sore throat? I was just waiting to deploy it for maximum effect. That noise? Oh, that's the alligators coming for you. Don't try to run. I have them very well trained.

CELLAR DOOR

I think about all that happened last year and whether I am haunted now, for life. What percentage of my life does that year constitute, and will that percentage shrink as I get older? What portion of my life will the grief of losing you consume? It feels like it has taken all of it right now. Your absence is sucking my life away, like a black hole. Will my life wrap around that year, your loss, like a pearl growing layers? It will be the grit of my life. Can my hurt be at the center of something that turns out to be beautiful or is it more likely that it will irritate me to the core of my being for the rest of my days? How astonishing that I have no way of answering this. I am not living right now. I am stuck here. I am still living in this house, Rowena.

The scariest thing I ever heard of before all this was a basement door that moved. I saw it on a television show once. Of course, I didn't see it actually move. The presenters of the show interviewed past inhabitants and they claimed that it moved. There was all sorts of claims in that show, the usual paranormal stuff: cold drafts and kids possessed and oil dripping down the walls and things that go bump in the night and flies at the windowsill, but that door is what got me. They showed it. They stood in the basement and filmed that ordinary-ass door. Come to think of it, it wasn't a door. It was just a doorway. A doorway, yes, an ordinary one in a basement, and they said that sometimes it moved. Sometimes that doorway was at the other side of the wall. From left to right, just switched over like that. I thought that it was one of the scariest things in the world. If things aren't fixed that way, if the way out or into somewhere can just move like that, then where does that leave us? Nothing can be sure then, nothing is fixed, and we may be trapped or locked out alternatively from our lives, from each other. That doorway means that everything is a lie.

Of course, this past year has shown me all of that is true. What scares me the most is true. That the reason I find that doorway so scary is because I know that it is true and I fear it.

Is this where I should begin? I don't think I'll be able to tell it straight or even slanted. I think I might have to circle around it, swirling like water down a sink until I hit the center, hit jackpot and go down the plughole.

Rowena, we were so stereotypical that it hurts. We got together in college, then after college moved in together and then talked about marriage maybe but realized that neither of us needed it, not really. We got our after-college jobs that we were way overqualified for and that didn't make a discernable dent in our student loans, but that was okay, everyone we knew was like that. We chugged along chugged along chugged along, squeezed ourselves into a tiny apartment. We talked about moving out, getting a bigger place, but with the rents in town it was impossible. We looked further and further afield, still impossible. Then realized that maybe buying might be cheaper, maybe. You asked your parents for help so we had a little bit of a deposit, then we looked at shack after shack after shack. Nothing that would work. We had no handywoman skills. Then, we saw the house on the hill. Set back in the woods, inexplicably cheap. Not in perfect condition, but perfect for us. My god. Had we not read the books and seen the movies? Had we (or rather, had I) not watched endless terrible paranormal TV shows? Where did you think I watched that door moving? Did we not joke about the Shirley Jackson reference? We did. And we did it anyway.

I once had my runes read when I was a teenager. I was at a youth group and this dude was there training or whatever, and he said he would read our runes for us. You could get away with that then. What did it say about me? He was just learning, he said. He said it was something to do with a farmer's wife and something to do with a nunnery. It didn't make much sense to me then. It doesn't make much sense to me now.

We stood holding hands on the threshold of our new home. We held hands that held the keys. We unlocked the door together. Stepped over the threshold. "Welcome home," you said.

"Welcome home," I said.

"Wait," you said. "Go back out again. I want to carry you over the threshold."

I bristled. "Why do you get to carry me?"

"Because you're smaller, dummy, and you have a bad back. Don't cut off your nose to spite your face."

"I'll do what I want," I said, but I let you carry me, grumbling.

The house wasn't anything extravagant. Our budget couldn't take something fancy, even at a severely reduced price. We couldn't believe our luck. No turrets or gothic features. No feature windows or ornate carvings. No brick. Not even an accessible attic. It was a smaller than average New England house, built in the '50s and not quite a ranch, not a Cape: a hybrid house with two small bedrooms, a lounge and an eat-in kitchen and a tiny basement with a dirt floor and extra steps that led to nowhere.

It needed a coat of paint, everywhere. So we had our friends over for a painting party before we moved the furniture in, and hired a local guy for the exterior. Everyone turned up at the same time, a Saturday, late summer when the air feels like September is on its way. The local guy frowned at our friends. He was courteous to us. We were paying him, after all. We went with classic white outside. I wanted black, but you said that was too dark. We couldn't agree on a color and beige makes me puke, so white it was, with black trim.

The outside painter man knew the house. "Had a lot of folks live here over the years," he said. "No one seems to stick." If he was hinting, we didn't get it. How stupid were we? Should've had *gullible* plastered all over our foreheads. So full of hope, we were, optimistic.

"Old man Cote built this, back in the day," he said. "My dad remembers him from when he was a kid. Scared the shit out of him, apparently. Near seven feet tall, hunchback. Heavy drinker. Worked at the old mill. Missing two fingers and a thumb from his left hand. Opened beer bottles with his teeth. You know the kind of guy."

No, I thought. *I don't. Should I?*

You were nodding. "Sounds like quite a guy," you said. "He built this place himself?"

"Him and a couple of buddies," said the painter guy. "It was how it was done back then. He lived alone here. Until he didn't. Live, I mean. Left it to his niece. She was a strange one. She'd lived in a nunnery and just left. Came and lived here alone too before building that house." He pointed next door, a bigger Cape. "She moved in there and sold this place. They rented it out after."

"She was a nun?" I said.

He shrugged. "I suppose so. I mean, if she lived in a nunnery. Who knows? All kinds of crazy stuff went on back then." He continued nodding as if answering himself, picked up his paint can and brushes and began slapping paint on the side of the house. We looked at each other, smirked, and went inside.

We moved our furniture in before the paint was quite dry. A couple of trips with a friend's truck was all it took. I let you arrange the furniture. You stood, lithe and stretching, in the kitchen. "Do you think it's okay if we put the dinner table over the basement hatch?"

"Yes," I said. "It's probably for the best." You laughed.

"Are you scared of the basement?"

"No," I said.

"Yes, you are. You're scared of all basements. It's not got a door, at least."

"It's got an *Evil Dead* hatch, for god sakes," I said. "Why did we buy this fucking house?"

"It's just a door in the floor," you said. "It won't harm you. Just try and ignore it. Do you remember that quote from *Donnie Darko* about 'cellar door' being the most beautiful phrase in the English language?"

"It was Tolkien," I said.

You reached your long arm out to me and held me to your chest.

That night you slept soundly in our new bedroom. I couldn't. I could hear every creak of the new house, every scratch of the trees on the roof. It was raining. I had new-homeowner terror. What if the roof leaked and we couldn't afford to fix it? Bankruptcy, losing the house, ruin. I saw an enormous white spider on the ceiling, walking back and forth, slowly in rows. "I'm having another LSD flashback," I said. You slept on.

What do I do with all these memories now that you're no longer here? I'm shouting them out into the ether, into nothing. I'm still talking to you, but you're gone. Is this more layers for this fucking pearl? If I keep talking, talking, talking, does that mean I build more layers? Is a memory retold cheating? Am I using the same events twice? Do they count more than once? I've been aware for some time that I might be crazy, but that's stereotypical in itself. All the crazy women are haunted. All women are crazy. We're hysterical, right? Howl at the moon.

Back in the olden days, doctors thought that all women's maladies were caused by a wandering uterus. The uterus was ambulatory, you see, and to be feared. It was not fixed in place. It could move anywhere: your knee, your wrist, your brain. It caused all kinds of trouble moving around. Is that what those male doctors feared? Men are scared of women they can't pin down.

Back in the apartment, before we got the house, we talked about our past sex lives. You had never dated a guy. Never. Pure lesbian, you said. I guffawed. Was I unpure, then? I'd dated guys before. Some of them were okay. What the hell was I? You're a lesbian passing bisexual, you said. You're very funny, I said. The word's *impure*, you said.

By the time we got that house we were locked in. Legally, financially, emotionally, sexually. We were ready to do this thing for life. I really believe that. We are not at fault here. Things occurred that were far bigger than we could control. It's not our fault.

When did it start, really? When did it begin? That first day with the painter guy and the old hunchback drunk and the nun? With the *Evil*

Dead basement and the stairs that went to nowhere? With you dead to the world in slumber and me seeing the ghost of acid trips past on the bedroom ceiling?

No, these are explainable, quantifiable. Of this world. Of this space and time. When did we start to slide off this axis?

The food. The food was the first thing. Everything we put in the fridge rotted. Everything. Within days. We had to get the guy from Randy's Appliances to come and look at it. He charged us fifty bucks but said it was fine. Still everything rotted. Onions would go green-black and collapse into each other in days. Cheese would grow hair in hours. Fruit? Forget it. It didn't stand a chance. I got a fruit bowl like my mother used to have, and even with the fruit flies it lasted longer outside of the fridge. We got another guy to look at it. Same. It was fine, he said. We ended up hauling it to the curb and giving it away. A couple of stoner kids from the neighborhood took it. When I asked them a month later, they said it worked fine (although I doubt they stored any real food in there). We bought a new fridge. Same. What fixed it? Moving the damn thing to the other side of the kitchen. Was it awkward there? Yes. You had to edge around it to get anywhere. Did it look ugly? Yes. But our food lasted long enough to eat, and I suppose that was the important thing. I've never had my stomach hurt as much as when we bought this house.

And yet, joy. This house has given me indescribable joy. I'm still here, even if you are not. Did you think I would leave? How could I? You might come back. I'd stand anything for the chance that you might come back. I can't afford to move, anyway. Remember what I vowed, all those times watching those stupid ghost shows, reading haunted house novels? I would never do what they do. When they recommend they sell the house? Then what, passing on a problem to someone else? Not dealing with your shit. That would make me as bad as the guy who sold us the house. What if it was a family with kids? I couldn't live with myself.

But.

Our house. OUR house. That we owned. That was cheaper than renting. Our house on the hill with our trees and love. My trees, my grove. I stood in the yard and watched the sun glimmer through the leaves and spun around and felt the sun on my face. I thanked the earth for these trees. I promised to look after them. You tried to plant stuff, flowers, geraniums, I think. You failed horribly, but I didn't care. I loved the dandelions that speckled what passed for a lawn. I loved the clover and fungi and ferns. Oh, what joy this place has given me. We could always eat takeout. Screw the fridge.

And next? Next next next. It's never linear. One thing happened after another, sure, but some things happened together and they were all in isolation. Am I attributing them to a cause that's in my mind? No. The ultimate question (or one of the ultimate questions) is, was it the house or me, or you even? I see a line of things happening temporally, but perhaps they were always happening all the time, and we just got a glimpse of them, like the scenes out the window of a train.

Let's reverse it. Wind it back. We were in college. You were from an even smaller town than me, but you'd lived in the city before. You seemed so together. I was flailing, just hanging on to my grades, in a life where I felt swallowed by the vastness of the city. I had run away from a small town, desperate for escape, convinced that I needed to get away, but then? I was a small fish in a big pond and I was forever diminishing. It was all too much. I was gauche and gawky, ripe to be taken advantage of by people worldlier but stupider than me. Then you swooped in. Sent me a drink at the bar, then came over to join me. It seemed almost chivalrous. We sat on bar stools, our faces reflected in the mirror behind the bar. You a head taller than me. Your short, bleached-blonde hair ruffled. I looked like a little dark-haired gremlin in comparison. You looked like an angel. You still do, or at least, I hope you still do. A row of silver earrings lining your ear instead of a halo. We went home together that night. You came over to my dorm room and we rarely slept apart again.

The yeast infections were the next part, I think. Once we moved into the house, you got a yeast infection that just wouldn't go away. "I'm foaming at the vagina," you'd say, and laugh, but I could tell by the twist of your lips, your frown when I wasn't looking, how physically irritated you were. You tried everything: over the counter stuff, what the doctor gave you. We didn't have health insurance, so when it got too expensive you made your own boric acid suppositories on the kitchen table, scooping the white powder tipped out on a magazine into non-gelatin vegan capsules.

"That's one expensive vagina," I'd joke, but it wasn't funny. None of it was. You didn't want me to touch you. You didn't want to touch me. It was too frustrating. You would snap at nothing, the irritation affecting everything.

We're a story, you and me. Everyone is. We're all stories. The difference between people is whether they're at the center of their own story or someone else is. I've always been the protagonist of my own story. I err on the side of self-absorption, narcissism, though my self-regard was malleable. You, though. You always looked out for everyone. The sidekick of your own narrative. Maybe I got it wrong. Maybe you were the star of your own show. Perhaps I was blinded by my own auto-idolatry. Now, though, you've taken center stage. You haunt my dreams. Last night I dreamt you hovered above me, your hair like a halo. You put your fingers to your lips as if to say "shush," and then you were gone.

I became convinced that the guy who had built the house, the super-tall hunchback guy, Mr. Cote, had died in our bathroom. I can't tell you how I knew, but I just did. I could feel him in there. Not totally present, not watching me in the shower or anything. He wasn't a creeper. I just always felt like if I pulled the shower curtain fast enough, I could maybe catch him. I'm a coward. I never whipped that shower curtain open quickly. But I strongly believe he died in there. Maybe of a heart attack in the bath? Maybe his liver failed. A lot of people die on the toilet, so I've heard. Death is not dignified. I felt the echo of him in there, his death throes. Was I scared? You know I'm a big baby about this kind of thing. I believed him harmless. I still do. He's not the one who caused the haunt, but I still felt a little scared when I would shower. I was uncomfortable. I didn't like to think of him experiencing that over and over. If that happens, is the ghost conscious of it, or is it like a record skipping? Remember records? They're back in fashion, apparently.

I tried to find out if my feelings were true. I tried to find his death record at the local library, at the town hall. I asked the older neighbors. No one could tell me. He'd died all right, people's relatives had remembered that, but very little else. There'd been a fire in the town hall 20 years ago. All the paper records were lost.

It didn't matter anyway. We cat-sat for Plutarch, our friend's big, black cat. Scary-looking, with big yellow eyes, but generally quite affectionate, for a cat. He loves you. Tolerates me. He spent a lot of time in the bathroom in the two weeks he was here. He would sit on the memory foam mat next to the heating vent. After that, Mr. Cote was gone. I've read on the internet that black cats have occult powers, that they can exorcize ghosts. Maybe Plutarch sent him to the light, or maybe Mr. Cote really fucking hated cats. Nevertheless, I was thankful. At least I could shower in peace. The bathroom became the only safe place in the house, a refuge.

I suppose I should talk about the steps to nowhere. We'd joked about them, of course. You knew how I felt about basements. I fucking hate all basements. There's nothing good about them. It's not like it happened right away. I mean, we settled in and got comfortable for the first couple of months. Sure, the fridge thing was weird and expensive, and the yeast infection thing was aggravating, but it was nothing too out of the ordinary. I know that my obsession with the old man and the thing with Plutarch was a bit weird, but nothing out of the realms of my own behavior in the past, if I'm honest about it. The stairs, though. This was some honest-to-god supernatural shit going on. The kind of thing that gets you invited on one of those shows where you tearfully tell your story, and they make sure to emphasize what a reliable witness you are and then get better-looking versions of you to reenact it.

The first time it happened, you had gone away for a conference. It was my first night alone in the house, but I wasn't worried. As I said, we were starting to get comfortable and you often had to go away for work. It was no big deal. I got in from work, had a light dinner, and then watched TV until bedtime. Nothing scary, not even my usual paranormal shows, just in case they spooked me. I just watched a talk show or two and went to bed early to read.

I wasn't asleep when it happened the first time. That's key, I think. I absolutely wasn't asleep. Later you tried to convince me that I was, that I was doing that thing where you nod off still reading, your eyes drooping down, then later you jerk awake and realize you can't remember the last couple of pages. I absolutely was not doing that. I know at the time it was easier to believe that I was.

I was awake and it was so fucking loud, so distinct, big thudding footsteps coming from one side of the house. Coming from the basement. Coming from the side of the basement that had steps to nowhere. Big thudding footsteps on wood. Wooden steps. It sounded like someone, definitely a person, and a big person at that, was walking up and down the cellar steps. It wasn't anything else. It wasn't the pipes knocking or a heating vent expanding and contracting or a tree limb scratching the roof. It was footsteps. My first thought was that it was an intruder.

I grabbed my phone off the nightstand and jabbed my head under the covers. I dialed your number, my breathing quick and shallow, using all of the good air in my duvet bubble. Your voice was sleepy and indistinct. I'd woken you up. "Rowena," I said, my voice harsh, whispering, "Rowena, there's an intruder in the house."

You woke up quickly. "What!? You need to call the police. Where is he?"

"I'm not sure. I mean, I am. Basement. Those stairs that go to nowhere." I was crying now.

"That doesn't make sense," you said. "They don't go anywhere, and he can't get in other than by going through the trap door. Have you been asleep? Could someone have broken in?" You took a sharp intake of breath. "It doesn't matter anyway. Karen, call the police. Can you still hear it?"

"I dunno," I said. I slowly poked my head out of the covers. I daren't open my eyes. What if the intruder was in my bedroom? I didn't want to see anything. But there was nothing. I opened my eyes. I brought my head up fully. There was nothing. Just the normal sounds of the house: the refrigerator humming, the heat switching on and the air coming out of the vents (it was fall by then). "It's...gone."

"Are you sure?"

"I can't hear anything."

"Go and check."

"Are you fucking kidding me?"

"I'll stay on the line. If anything happens, I'll call the police."

"That doesn't sound like a plan."

"Can you hear anything?"

"No."

"Are you sure you weren't asleep?"

"I am wide awake."

I slid out of bed and crept into the other room. I switched the light on. Nothing. I went through all the rooms. Nothing was amiss. "There's no one here."

"What about in the cellar?"

"There is absolutely no fucking way I am going down in that basement alone. I'd rather just go back to bed and wait to be murdered."

You chuckled. "Okay then, but keep your phone on the nightstand." I got back to sleep, eventually, and slept more soundly than I had any right to.

The next time it happened, you were here.

It was late again; we were both in bed. I was asleep this time, but you were staying up a bit later, watching Netflix on your tablet. You shook me awake. "Karen," you whispered. "Listen." There it was again. Heavy footsteps on the stairs to nowhere in the basement.

"It's the same as before," I whispered. "It's coming from those cellar steps."

"HELLO!" you shouted. I nearly jumped out of my skin.

"Shhhh," I said. "They'll hear you."

"Who will?" you said. The footsteps continued. "Fuck this, I'm going out to check. Are you coming?" I stayed, frozen, as you climbed out of bed and pulled on your robe. You've always been braver than me. As soon as you opened the bedroom door, it stopped. You poked your head out the door, then pulled it back in and looked at me. "Come on, let's go investigate." I got out of bed and threw my robe on too. We walked through the house, holding hands. You went first, flicking every light on as we went. There was no one there. We checked out all of the windows, flicked the outdoor lights on. Nothing. "There's only one place left to look," you said, and nodded your head at the trap door under the table.

"Oh no," I said. "I'm not going down there."

"Come on," you said. "Don't make me go down alone. I'm pretty sure that's where it's coming from. Please don't leave me to be murdered alone." You wrapped your arms around me. I sighed.

"Come on, then, but you go first and let me get my phone to use the flashlight."

"There's a light down there."

"I want a flashlight too. Plus, what if we have to call the police?" I could see that any fear that you had on hearing the footsteps was dissipating. I went and grabbed my phone.

The table was heavy and needed two of us to lift it. We picked it up and moved it to the other side so we could open the trapdoor.

As we pulled the trapdoor open, dust motes filled the air and the stale smell of the basement rose up and assaulted our nostrils. I flicked the flashlight setting on my phone, almost too scared to point towards the open maw of the trapdoor. I pointed it down briefly; just the steps and the dirt floor were illuminated as the light swung in an arc. "Keep it still," you said. "Having you swing it about is worse than having no light." I trained the beam on the bottom of the steps.

"Hold my hand," I said. You held your hand out to me and slowly we descended the basement steps. I kept the light studiously in front of our feet, only ensuring we wouldn't fall. I did not want to look. I never wanted to look. I fucking hate basements.

You reached out your other hand and pulled the string to turn on the single bulb that was the only light in the basement. As it clicked on, I instinctively closed my eyes. "I don't want to see," I said. You paused. I waited, listening to my own breathing, ragged and scared, and then your hot breath on my face.

"There's nothing. It's fine. Open your eyes, darling." You laughed. I opened my eyes. You were right. There was nothing unusual about the basement. The furnace, the half-filled paint cans, the plastic box of Christmas ornaments, and in the corner, the steps to nowhere, crouching like a sulking animal.

"It's not fine, though," I said. "You heard those footsteps. They were coming from over there." I pointed to the steps. "Why are those steps there?" You broke away from my hand; I panicked and grasped the air behind you. You walked over to the steps, looked above your head, and poked the low ceiling. "It looks like it was boarded up."

"Maybe a previous owner wanted more floor space, or, it looks like it went outside. Maybe they didn't want a bulkhead. Perhaps animals kept getting in. There's got to be a logical explanation."

I sighed. "I suppose you're right. Come on, let's go to bed." You came back over, turning off the light bulb on your way. I let you go past me on the stairs, holding up the phone to light your way. As I began walking up the steps myself, there was a loud huff in my left ear, a breath that was cold and as icy as yours had been warm. I whipped my body around, the phone light swinging with me. I lost my footing and wobbled down a couple of steps, twisting my ankle. "Who's there?" I shouted, my voice shaking. There was nothing. I scrabbled up the stairs backwards, knocking you onto the kitchen floor.

"It was probably a draft," you said later as we lay in bed.

"Probably," I said, but I knew it wasn't.

After that, my dreams changed. I found us on the cellar steps, over and over again. You were saying, "There's nothing. There's nothing there." And I could clearly see that there was something, dark and swirling, almost like a black hole in the corner of the basement next to the steps.

"It's over there," I said, and pointed, but you refused to look that way. You would look everywhere else apart from where the black mass was.

"There's nothing," you said, over and over again. Then I felt a pull from the swirling mass, like it was drawing me in, sucking me towards it. I tried to hang on to you but you let go of my hand. I could feel my feet starting to slip so I grabbed onto the bannister of the steps. The pull got stronger and stronger, my feet sliding on the dirt floor as I tried to gain purchase. With both hands on the bannister, I hung on for dear life. I screamed your name but you ignored me. You continued to look anywhere but at the hole and told me it was nothing. My feet lost traction and I slammed to the ground, the shock of it loosening my grip. I slid towards the hole, but still you didn't notice, and when I got there I saw it was black, viscous liquid, like oil.

It sucked me in, first my feet and legs, then my torso, my clothes stained inky black. Soon it had my hands and arms and finally my head. I was choking on the black liquid, drowning. When I woke up, I was coughing, my body drenched in sweat.

I reached out to you, touched your back, grateful that it was all a dream. I lay back, closed my eyes. I'm back in the cellar again with you. I spend my nights doing this over and over again. I'm still dreaming it, even though I know how it ends and when I reach out to you, there's just empty air.

The black patch on the bedroom ceiling and the sleepwalking started together, I think. Mold, concentrated in the corner, spreading out in concentric circles. My homeowner anxieties coming to fruition. I'm allergic to mold. The one thing I had insisted on was a house inspection. The inspector had shrugged. "I don't see any mold, but I can't get into that roof space so I can't say for certain." You rising in the night like the bride of Dracula, climbing out of the sheets, eyes closed, purposeful slow walk of a movie monster. I called your name but nothing would register. "Row, Row, Rowena." My voice getting louder, but you didn't acknowledge me. So I followed, feeling like I was intruding on something private. Into the kitchen, you grabbed and shifted the table like it was nothing and then started grabbing at the trapdoor, scratching at the ring to pull it up, your hands claws. You woke up, your blue eyes filled with confusion.

"Where am I, Karen?" I pulled you into my arms.

"You're at home. Just sleepwalking. It's okay." I walked you back to bed.

We couldn't get someone to look at the ceiling. They were all booked up—busy time of year, apparently. It didn't matter anyway. Within a week, the rot had gotten so bad that the drywall was dropping, mushy. It fell through and revealed the culprit—a mouse nest, filled with a mouse family that had died of some unknown cause. You took them out and laid them in the woods. We got the outside painter guy to come and fix up the hole. Once he'd cut away the tainted pieces of boards, he stuck his head up through the hole.

"I suppose there's no other way up here. Want to look before I close it off again?"

I shook my head. "No."

"Oh, come on, Karen," you said. "I thought it was basements you didn't like. Has it now expanded to attics?"

"What if there's mold?"

"Doesn't look moldy," said the handyman. "Looks a bit dry, if anything."

"I'll have a look," you said. He moved out of the way so you could stand on the ladder and poke your head through. "Nothing to see," you said. "Just a regular old attic—stale air and insulation and"—you sneezed—"dust. Here, I'll take some photos." You pulled your phone out of your pocket and lifted it through the hole. Of course, there was something to see, later. In every photo, in just one corner, a hulking dark mass scowling back at us. "Dust on the lens," you said, but I knew you didn't believe it.

The footsteps on the basement stairs were loud that night.

So the other thing you should probably know is that I'm fairly sure that your parents think I've murdered you. It would be funny if they weren't so damn earnest about it. I've had to lie to them, obviously. I've always been a terrible liar; you know that, so there's no wonder they're suspicious. I told them that you had left me for another woman. Don't get mad. I didn't think it through, and I was trying to make sure they didn't call the police. I couldn't tell them the truth, could I? You ran away with Susan, I said. I said I thought she might be Canadian. I said I assumed you would contact them when you were settled. Not a good long-term plan, I admit, but I wasn't thinking. At that point, I was still hopeful that you would return. I still am hopeful. No, I want to be hopeful. I feel like if I stop pretending to be hopeful, then I'll jinx us and then you really truly will be gone. You'll never come back if I give up my fake hope. Work was easy. What are we but fancy temps? They replaced you in no time, and yes, I hate him already. Your parents, though. They're not so easily assuaged. At first they were coming over every couple of days. They said to "check on me," ostensibly, but that wasn't all of it, of course. I found your mom going through our drawers. "What didn't she take her things?" she said. I shrugged. At least I didn't have to fake my grief. That was real enough. I stood there hollow-eyed as she pulled your shirt to her face and breathed in your scent, just as I had done not an hour earlier. I swear I caught your dad poking around in the yard, maybe looking for a burial. They did contact the police, who came over. I gave them the same story. They told your parents that you were an adult and you left on your own free will and there wasn't much they could do about it. I know they're still trying. I think they've declared you as missing, which is not wrong. They call me every month now, and we rehash the story over and over. It almost feels true. I fucking hate imaginary Susan, that bitch.

The sleepwalking got worse. Every night, *every night*, I would wake up, find you scratching at the *Evil Dead* door in the kitchen floor. It always happened around 3 a.m. Around the same time, we would hear the footsteps, if it happened. Always 3 a.m. Between my nightmares and your somnambulism, I was wrecked. I couldn't concentrate at work; our eating was terrible; we were both too tired to cook. I began sleeping through your nightly wanderings, only waking when you had opened the trapdoor and were halfway down the steps. You started talking, too. "I have to get to the door, Karen," you would say.

"What door?" I said. "The cellar door? It's back there." You ignored me.

"I have to find the door," you said. "I have to find it." Then you would wake up confused. When I asked you about the door, you claimed you didn't know anything about it. "I must be dreaming," you said. "I don't remember anything."

Remember when I went for that Reiki session? I'd won a free session from a raffle at work. You, ever the rationalist, laughed at me.

"Going for some magic spells?" you said. I went anyway. It was free and you never know, right? I didn't feel anything when she did it. I tried to relax, tried to feel something, but nothing. After we had finished, the woman said, "I felt your trauma. I saw it pour out from the soles of your feet. Old, dark blood. Old trauma you have hung on to for too long. The dark blood comes from the feet." I thanked her, awkwardly. I felt like she really believed, even if I didn't. "There's someone watching over you," she said, as I walked out the door. "She looks like a nun. She has a gray scarf over her head." I didn't hear any more. As I walked out into the bright sunlight of the parking lot, the full heat of summer beating down, I began to freeze. A cold sweat enveloped my body, and I didn't warm up until long after I arrived home.

I miss you so much, Row. I miss you so much it's like a hole in my chest that will never heal. It makes it hard to breathe. Sometime my fake hope falters. If I imagine the worst, then maybe the universe or whoever is in charge of this fucking thing will not think me arrogant for assuming you will come back to me, and then maybe they'll give you back. I can't leave here just in case, though, so my stupid arrogance is still there, my stupid hope. It's getting so bad, Rowena. The footsteps are every night, louder and louder, and the mold, oh, the mold, black streaks snaking up the walls. No matter how much I wash it down with bleach, it's too much. The doctor gave me an inhaler, but I daren't confess that I knew the cause. I have your yeast infections now. It's all through my body. I've been taking the antifungals the doctor gave you when we finally had to spend all our money on medical appointments. You said they didn't work and you were right. I can see white spots forming on the inside of my cheeks. I dream about the thing in the attic, hulking there, watching over the whole house malevolently. I miss Mr. Cote. Maybe it would have been better if he stayed. I wonder if I'm going crazy...crazier. I look through the photos on my phone to check that you existed. But if you were a figure of my imagination, then I could imagine photos too, right? Every time your parents visit, they try to not notice the mold, the decay of the house, the rotting food everywhere, the smell. They look at me with pity and suspicion.

You started to go down to the basement when you were awake. You'd get home from work before me, and I would walk in to the table set askew, the floor hatch open. "Row," I'd shout, not wanting to go down there. "Rowena, what are you doing?"

"Nothing," you'd say. "Just storing some stuff." But it happened more and more, and I started going down to see what you were doing. You would always jump up when I came down the steps, start bustling. Finally, I managed to sneak down without you noticing. You weren't doing much, just sitting on the dirt floor cross-legged, facing the steps to nowhere in silence. When I asked what you were doing, you jumped up. then looked confused. Your confusion turned to anger. "Fucking spying on me now," you said, and pushed past me roughly as you climbed the stairs back to the kitchen. I hurried after you, afraid to be in the basement on my own.

Remember when we first found all the kitchen cupboard doors open? All the cups on the counter, face-down. How we blamed each other? Even laughed a little? I just leave them there now. They've won. Whatever they wanted to say, they've said it. I don't have any control over this house anymore. Maybe I never did. I never did, Row.

Shall we talk about when you left? I go through the steps of it all the time. Trying to find a way that maybe I could have saved you. Is "saved" the right word even? I mean, you walked right into it. That's what torments me the most. Maybe you wanted to go, wanted to go for good. Maybe you wanted to leave, and if that's the case then you're never coming back. My hopes for your return all hinge on the idea that if you could make it back to me, you would. You would, right, Rowena? What is worse: imagining you stuck in that place, wherever or whatever it is, or imagining that you would leave me here alone? Nothing is right and nothing doesn't hurt.

It was 3 a.m. again. You sleepwalked to the kitchen. This I assume, as I was still asleep. When I woke, I knew immediately that you weren't there and I made my way to the kitchen. The steps on the stairs to nowhere were loud, thundering. I was terrified, but I had to look for you. The table was on its side. I still don't know if you had tipped it over. I'd have thought you weren't strong enough, but who knows. Why didn't the noise of it falling wake me up? The fridge was open, the milk on its side, already sour as it spread across the floor. The cupboards were open and the cups put out, face-down on the counter again. I made my way down the basement steps shouting your name. I switched the light on, petrified. There you were. Standing in front of the steps in your nightshirt, bare feet dirty from the floor. At the top of the steps, a door. A door that had never been there before. A fucking ordinary-looking, solid fucking door, wood, painted white but dirty and peeling. Not quite the open doorway of my obsession, but fucking close enough. The obscenity of it—a door that didn't fucking exist before, there, solid, taunting me with its reality. Your hand reaching out to the doorknob. Me screaming, "No!" From under the door, blackness like oil seeping through and running down the steps, just like my dream. I saw it touch your toes and begin to cover your feet and ankles. My fear freezing me in place. Acid bile rising up my throat that I puked instantly onto the floor. You touched that doorknob, it turned, and the door opened to blackness. You stepped through it and that was the last time I saw you.

There is no Susan. You haven't left me for her. You're not even dead. How can I explain this to anyone, Row? Once it had swallowed you, the door disappeared. I haven't seen it again since.

I spend my days sitting at the bottom of these hated basement steps, gulping down my fear. I drink too much and don't look after myself. The house is collapsing around me, controlled by a force that I believe sees me as its nemesis. I wait for the door to reappear. I wait for you to come back. When are you coming back, Row?

WHITECHAPEL

The tops of her thighs wobble as she skips down Whitechapel Road. Her skin is so white it gleams as it escapes from under her denim hotpants. I walk behind her to watch. She keeps looking around to check I can see her. Her face is just as pale, a slash of red on her mouth, pearly teeth smiling. She pokes her tongue out at me, pink and slippery and just suggestive enough to make me groan inwardly. She knows I'll follow her anywhere. She's been attracting looks since we arrived in London, but here it is more noticeable. Whitechapel is predominately Bangladeshi these days, its women devout Muslim and covered. Lola looks like a streetwalker in comparison, bare legs and bellybutton, her black shirt cut low and her sooty eyelashes fluttering. Her hennaed hair sways as she skips, and her nails are varnished and chipped. Some of the men openly stare. No one sees me, the tall, skinny boy trailing after her.

We met in our first year of college. I'd come from an all-boy prep school, so even a small East Coast college was a shock. I hid behind stone arches, sat at the back of the lecture hall and in the corner of the dining room. The girls were so full of themselves, so strident and confident. I couldn't talk to them. I was hiding behind a tree watching everyone sit on the grass of the quad when there was a voice behind me.

"Don't they all fucking think they're something." She was like nothing I had ever seen, leaning against the Commons steps. Her hair was black then, glossy and thick. She wore tight jeans and a figure-hugging shirt; all of the other girls seemed anemic and bland in comparison. She was smoking a cigarette, a kiss of red lipstick around the filter. "Every single one of them thinks the world revolves around them, just like their parents told them. Means the rest of us have to suffer listening to them." I looked over at them, all laughing at their in-jokes. She was right. "Leave them to it, is what I say." She took a drag of her cigarette and blew the smoke into the air. "Why are you hiding behind a tree?" she said. I couldn't speak to her, just shrugged. "Come on, where does a girl go to get a drink around here?" We'd been inseparable ever since, or rather, she did what she always did and I came along too.

This trip to Europe was her idea. Everything we do is her idea. She sprawled across my dorm bed in a black dress despite the early summer heat, her head dangling over the end of the bed while I sat on the floor facing her, back against the wall. She had a hangover, bluish smudges under her eyes. We were supposed to be studying for finals.

"After next year, we'll be adults, Toby," she said. "Might as well be dead. Once college is over, we'll have to get actual jobs. I'll end up in some office, my soul dying to pay off my student loans." We both knew I wouldn't be paying off student loans or getting a crappy job. She didn't say as much, but it was there in the implication. My family has money, old money. They ignore me, mostly. I would go to grad school, probably reading law, then pretend to work for the family business. "Let's go to Europe, Toby." She rolled over so her head was facing the right way up. "This summer, let's go see some real death." She propped up her chin with her hands. I could see down her dress; she had no bra on. I nodded. No question who would be paying. Instead of studying, she plotted our route on Google Maps and printed it out. Before she pinned it to my corkboard, she wrote "Lola and Toby's Death Tour" in black swirly writing, hearts around our names.

We started in Pripyat, Ukraine, where Chernobyl exhaled its poison. They tell you not to step on the moss there, as it absorbs the radiation more than anything. There are old women who still live on the tainted land, eating radioactive cabbage as if nothing happened. We looked at concrete apartment blocks that nature had reclaimed, trees bursting through empty windows. Lola cooed over abandoned cradles and dolls with sunken faces, chased after the packs of dogs descended from family pets and bred with wolves. It felt like we were the last people in the world. She said it looked just like *Fallout*. I tried to kiss her under the Ferris wheel, but she laughed and ran away, linking arms with a German tourist we had met at the hotel.

At Auschwitz, we looked solemn as we walked through the death camps. Lola's eyes were large and sympathetic as she looked at the tour guide. I wondered whether it was a lie, her sympathy. What was it she really felt under that mask of sorrow? Did she feel for these people that were treated so horribly? I tried to imagine what it was like to be taken to the gas chambers, but all I could think of was the night before when she had let me lie on the bed next to her instead of on the floor like I usually did. She was under the covers and I was on top of them, but I was still there close to her. I thought about her sleeping, her eyes closed and her breath on my face as we walked through the gas chambers, and I felt guilty, bad for all those who didn't breathe anymore.

This morning, we walked around Highgate Cemetery. Lola wanted to see where the Rossettis were buried, but that was in West Cemetery and we hadn't booked ahead for the tour. We went to East Cemetery instead. At the gate, a man stopped us and told us that Lola had to cover up her shoulders. I gave her my plaid shirt, but she sulked as we walked through the monuments. She stood in the green shafts of light filtering through the trees among the angels and Celtic crosses. With the warm red of my shirt brushing her cheek and her sullen lips, I'd never seen her look so beautiful. I tried taking a photo of her with my phone, but she refused, still angry with me. I just wanted to capture her, keep her there forever. We looked at Karl Marx's tomb, his huge head on a plinth, but we had no sympathy for the working man. My favorite was the bare-knuckle fighter's with his loyal dog standing guard, the chief mourner at his funeral. I told Lola we should learn from that dog, but she scoffed. The only grave she was taken by was the pop art painter's, with the word "dead" in block letters. Only then would she consent to a photograph, but she wouldn't look into the lens.

><><

After Poland, we went to see the Sedlec Ossuary, just outside Prague. Inside, the small chapel is decorated with hundreds of human skeletons. I had vertigo standing under the huge chandelier made of bones. "It's beautiful," Lola said, and squeezed my hand. We stayed in a confection of a hotel with a view of the astronomical clock. We wandered through the gothic streets of the Old Town, getting drunk in the cafes and talking about Kafka. We said we'd move here after college, wear heavy coats as we walked across the Charles Bridge. This was the old world, where we belonged; we would leave the plastic, McFried America behind. I'd never been happier. Fuzzy with absinthe, she let me touch her night after night. As she slept, I told her I loved her.

We were never a couple in college, although people assumed we were. Lola consumed most of my life; I never dated or had any real friends. She eschewed female friends and chose her lovers from the town next to the college, monosyllabic men with dirt underneath their fingernails: musicians, mechanics, bartenders. None of them lasted long. I waited, and hoped.

><><

In the romantic city of Paris, she turned cold again. She started talking about college, and our final year.

"What am I going to do, Toby?" she said. "What am I fucking qualified to do for all my fancy learning? Give blow jobs at the back of bars? It's what I do best. I could have done that without a college degree." What could I say? "Stop wincing, Toby, you've got nothing to worry about." And then she stopped and smirked. "What's a-matter? You upset I never gave you one?" I walked away from her, back to the hotel. She was contrite that night when she came back, the sting of cognac on her lips. The next day we held hands as we explored the Paris Catacombs, lingering at the back of the tour group.

Now we are in London, our final stop before we return to the States. I'm back on the hotel room floor again, though she doesn't explain why. We've visited the Tower and the Dungeons and Highgate, but here we are in the place where Lola wanted to be the most. The morning mood of the cemetery forgotten, she skips and laughs through Whitechapel, the art galleries and mosques giving little clue to the hamlet's previous incarnation. Our first destination is Durward Street, although it wasn't always called that. These London streets are slippery. They aren't what they say they are, and they used to be something else. I wonder if Lola used to be something else, before I met her. She appeared to me fully formed, but she can't have always been this way. I've never seen a childhood picture, and she never talks about her parents. I'm not even sure if Lola is her real name. Toby isn't even my name. It's a name that Lola gave me. It says *Tiberius* on my birth certificate, along with a list of fancy family names. Lola didn't want to take the tour this time so we head out alone, but the sun is going down and I think we're safer than we would have been back then; still, we're a long way from home. Lola doesn't sense danger, she never has. We find our destination and Lola turns into the back street. There's nothing much to see: red brick buildings and parked vehicles, the smell of car exhaust. Lola stops and stares at the sidewalk.

"It was here," she said. "The first one, the first canon one." I look at her, but I can't read her face. "Mary Ann Nichols, throat cut left to right, just like the others." She mimics it by drawing a line across her throat with her finger. Her eyes are glittering. Is this what she came for? All the sights we've seen, all the death, has any of it satisfied her? "Abdomen mutilated, but not as bad as the rest." She stares at the ground.

"Where next, Lola?" I say. She consults her map.

"Hanbury Street." I follow her; she has a better sense of direction.

It's not far. The sun is nearly down. She stops in the road again; ordinary shop fronts and streetlamps. People walking up the road have to swerve to miss her. "Annie Chapman," she says, "throat cut from left to right, disemboweled, her intestines thrown over her shoulders. He took part of her uterus." I wish she would look at me the way she's looking at the pavement right now. There's a light inside her, showing through her eyes. Her voice is husky, trance-like. "13 Miller's Court."

She doesn't skip now. The light has faded. I can see the gooseflesh on the tops of her arms. We go under an archway and stand in a cobbled yard. We're alone and the sky is that deep blue just before dark. If we were inside, the outside would look like night, but our eyes are accustomed to the darkness. Lola points up to a window. "Mary Jane Kelly, last canon. He had a room. He took his time."

"Lola," I say. She blinks in the darkness, the light from the windows illuminating her face. She looks tired.

"He cut off her breasts and thighs, threw her internal organs around the room."

"Lola," I say.

"He mutilated her face. She was unrecognizable."

"Hey, Lola."

She looks at me. "He took away her heart." She clutches at her chest.

"Lola, what do you want?"

"Next is Henriques Street, Elizabeth Stride, then Mitre Square, Catherine Eddowes."

"And then what?"

"Hotel, home, college."

I grab hold of her chin and pull her face close to me. "Lola, what do you really want?"

She looks at me. "I want to feel alive." I let go of her face and she looks at her feet. And I know that she is already dying, that just existing in this world will suck the life out of girls like Lola. I realize I can do this; I can give her what she wants. I can save her. This one time, I can satisfy her. I take the straight razor from my pocket, the one I bought from Bond Street this morning while she still slept. I will slash left to right, canon, and get to work on the rest. I hold the blade above her, try and catch the light with it; my hand shakes as I grip it.

"Lola, it's time," I say, and I don't believe it myself as I'm saying it. She looks up, and for the first time I can see the little girl she might have been. Her eyes widen with horror.

"Toby, what the fuck are you doing?" She starts to back away, falls on the cobbles and begins to skitter backwards.

"It's what you want," I say, and I'm crying. "I can give you what you want, Lola."

She continues to move backwards like a crab, her heels skidding. She's crying too, black lines down her cheeks. "I don't want this. I was playing. Toby, please."

I drop the razor and sink to the floor, my knees jarring on the large round stones as I crumble. And as I try to breathe, sobbing as the adrenaline ebbs away, she crawls over to me and wraps her arms around me, her wet cheek against my head.

"Let's go home, Toby."

THE TALE OF BOBBY RED EYES

D*own **the lane and over** the hill*
Up the cinder path and through the trees

Find the tunnel mouth and go inside

Bobby Red Eyes, Bobby Red Eyes, Bobby Red Eyes

When did we learn this? It was always there from the time we started school, even before. Someone's older sister who was told by a young aunt who knew someone who knew someone else. Everyone had a link to Bobby. We'd chant it in the schoolyard, whisper it to each other at sleepovers, tell each other that Bobby Red Eyes would get us if we told a secret.

The dirt lane that led to the cinder path was at the top of our street next to the cornfields beyond. At harvest, the farmers would leave a hay bale for the kids so we'd leave the rest alone (it never worked). One year, my brother fell asleep in one and the entire neighborhood looked for him for hours, fearing he had been stolen. Stranger danger was what our parents were most afraid of, but we knew better. Bobby was scarier. At least once a year someone set fire to the cornfield, and it would spread to the fences of the houses nearest to the fields. We would stand and watch the red glow until the heat was too much. One year, one of the house's plastic windowsills melted.

Bobby was a kid who got run over by the train. Bobby was never a kid, but a demon pretending to be a kid. Bobby died in a fire in a house that used to be there before the tunnel. Bobby is a story kids tell other kids around here because there's nothing better to do.

There was nowhere else to go. We were allowed on the lane and no further. When someone said, "Let's go to the tunnel," we didn't give it a second thought. We had too much time on our hands and nothing to do. The tunnel was miles away, but we wouldn't be called to supper for hours. Our parents would never know. We'd cover each other.

In late summer, the path was hardened and cracked by the sun. We skipped down there, shouting and hollering and calling each other cruel names. Then the embankment at the end of the lane. The bravest took the quickest, steepest route and slid on their butts down the incline, dusty jean pockets for the rest of the way. That wasn't me; I took the gentler route to the broad black cinder path that had once been a railway track, its sleepers long gone. We were quieter here and talked with heads bent towards each other. For a mile, we walked up the black road.

Bobby was a kid like us who got murdered in the woods. They buried him in the tunnel. If you say "Bobby Red Eyes" three times in the mirror on Halloween, he'll be your reflection. Bobby murders animals and leaves them in the tunnel. Bobby never existed, he's just an urban legend.

Down the lane and over the hill

Up the cinder path and through the trees

Find the tunnel mouth and go inside

Bobby Red Eyes, Bobby Red Eyes, Bobby Red Eyes

By the time we got to the trees, we were silent. A miniature forest had sprung up between the embankments. The tree trunks were twisted and the limbs broken, boughs hanging low. We walked single file, bent double under the branches. By afternoon, we were tired but at the point of no return. Another half-mile through the trees, crawling in places, our hair snagged and arms scratched, hot, itchy bug bites covering us. Incongruous items half-glimpsed in the woods: an old washing machine, a burnt-out car, a rolled hay bale rotting, a tangled orange net. Towards the end, on hands and knees for the last section of the woods, I could smell the dead air of the tunnel. I wanted to go back, go home, but there was literally no turning. Trees on either side, and another couple of kids behind me. If I had been the last kid, would I have turned back? Probably not. Peer pressure is a powerful thing, and to go through the woods, down the isolated cinder road alone? That was nearly as scary as facing the tunnel. The sun was on its way down. A cold breeze snaked through the trees and chilled our sweaty, itchy skin.

Bobby's not a kid, he was a signalman like the one in the story. Bobby was a soldier who never came back from the war. Bobby is a kid, he fell off the top of the tunnel and got run over by a train. Only babies believe in Bobby—ghost stories are for kids.

Down the lane and over the hill

Up the cinder path and through the trees

Find the tunnel mouth and go inside

Bobby Red Eyes, Bobby Red Eyes, Bobby Red Eyes

The trees opened up and we stared into the screaming black mouth of the tunnel, made of blackened brick and covered in faded, spray-painted graffiti from the seventies. I shivered but I wasn't cold. The locals call it the mile tunnel. There's a tiny semi-circle of light at the end. I started to back away into the trees. One kid had already been in the tunnel once. "There's dead dogs in there," he said. "If your dog goes missing, this is where it is. Drowned in the red ochre. There's a massive pool of it halfway through. Don't step in it or it'll suck you under." I knew what red ochre was. My terrier Brandy was impossible to keep in the yard. He'd once come home covered in the thick red clay. Had my little dog come down here and managed to get out again?

"It'll get dark soon," I said. "Maybe we should turn back."

If you see two red eyes looking at you as you lie in bed, it's Bobby telling you you'll join him soon. No, if you see two red eyes and say, "Bobby Red Eyes, you can't catch me," then you'll be fine. No, "Bobby Red Eyes, you can't catch me" will bring the red eyes but you're safe 'cos you called him. It's probably the red lights from your stereo, stupid. Bobby doesn't exist.

They were all already making their way in, and what could I do? I didn't want to get left behind. We walked in the middle of the cavernous tunnel, built to allow two steam trains with plenty of room, cut into the countryside to keep the rail flat. We shied away from the edges that had niches every 100 feet so that workers could flatten themselves against brick-lined safety when a train came roaring past. These dark nooks were the perfect place for Bobby to hide, to reach out a pale arm and drag someone in. We avoided them. Soon we were running out of light. "Let's go back and try another day," I said. I was ignored. We linked arms and continued walking in the middle. The cinder path had ended. Now it was trampled-down dirt. When someone stumbled in the dusky light, we pulled them up. I was at the end. Not popular enough to have two arms comforting mine.

Bobby was a kid who didn't have any friends, so he jumped in front of a train. Bobby was pushed in front of the train by bullies. Bobby was the bully and he fell. Bobby was a kid who died, but he's not haunting the mile tunnel.

The further we walked, the more uneven the ground was. The air was getting even staler and there was barely any light left, just the darkening semi-circle at the end of the tunnel, still so far away. A kid started singing, tried to get the others to join in. No one took him up on his offer and his thin, reedy voice died in the darkness. Soon we couldn't see what was right in front of us. The same kid started whistling the funeral march. Someone told him to shut up. The rest of the kids laughed and made ghost noises. A girl in the middle shouted, "I just saw red eyes!" She screamed, but it wasn't a real one. It was the squealing of a girl used to getting attention.

Down the lane and over the hill

Up the cinder path and through the trees

Find the tunnel mouth and go inside

Bobby Red Eyes, Bobby Red Eyes, Bobby Red Eyes

"We must be somewhere near the middle now," someone said.

"Watch out for red ochre," said another.

"How can we do that?" said the other kid at the end of the line. "It's pitch black."

There was twittering above us, a suggestion of movement. "It's just bats," said another kid. The squealy girl started up again. She had long hair. Everyone knew that bats tangled themselves in long hair. "That's just a myth," said the bat kid. The girl with the long hair still whimpered. We trudged along. The floor got wetter and stickier at our feet. A damp chill moved over us. Water drops echoed off the walls. Our forward movement was unstoppable now. We didn't have a plan. Were we really going to the end? If we did that, then what? No one had thought of that. Who would call their parents to pick us up from the country road near where the mile tunnel ended? We'd all get in trouble for sure.

The mile tunnel is a portal to Hell. The mile tunnel was built over a graveyard. They left the bones. The mile tunnel was once filled with poison gas that killed some of the workers. No, when they were building the tunnel some workers died from exhaustion. They bricked their bodies up inside the walls. The mile tunnel is an old, disused railway tunnel that isn't structurally safe.

It got harder and harder to walk. The red ochre sucked at our feet at every step, getting deeper each time. Soon it was oozing, cold and thick, over the tops of my sneakers. "Let's go back," I said. "We have to be more than halfway now."

"My brother said that once you get past the red ochre, it's easy," said the whistling kid. "Might as well keep going."

"Yeah, Roberta," sneered someone else. "Don't be a chicken." Ankle deep now, I kept trudging, pulling on the arm of the next kid.

The red ochre is a mark. Once you get it on you, you're Bobby's forever. The red ochre is actually the blood of the workers mixed with mud. Wrong. It's dogs' blood, so many dead dogs. Bobby lives in the mud. He's the one that drags the dogs down. Red ochre is just iron oxide in the dirt. It's wet because of the conditions in the tunnel.

Soon I was up to my knees in red ochre. Was it happening to the others? They seemed to be moving much more easily than me. Then they started, was it the bat kid, the squealy girl with long hair, the whistler? It was too hard to tell. They began chanting, laughing as they did:

Down the lane and over the hill

Up the cinder path and through the trees

Find the tunnel mouth and go inside

Bobby Red Eyes, Bobby Red Eyes, Bobby Red Eyes

The chain of arms broke apart like a string of pearls snapping. The rest of the kids ran back where we came from. I heard their feet squelching and then slap-echoing as they got to firmer ground. They were shouting, "Roberta, come on! You've got to run." But I couldn't. I was up to my thighs in cold, gritty mud and every move I made, to turn, to free my legs and feet, made me sink deeper and deeper. I fell forward and my arms plunged into the red ochre. I couldn't see anything, just blackness. It was pulling me under, sucking me down. Now to my waist, my elbows. I couldn't hear the others. They were long gone. Now to my shoulders and neck. I twisted my head to try and breathe, but it was no use. Soon it was over my nose and mouth and filling my eyes, covering the top of my head.

Down the lane and over the hill

Up the cinder path and through the trees

Find the tunnel mouth and go inside

Bobby Red Eyes, Bobby Red Eyes, Bobby Red Eyes

Bobby was a girl who thought she had friends but didn't. Bobby disobeyed her parents and walked down the cinder path. Bobby was abandoned by neighborhood kids and drowned in the red ochre. Bobby was a kid who went missing in the mile tunnel. Bobby never existed, she is just a story.

DEVOUR

He slammed the knife down, sticking the eight-inch blade in the coffee table, leaving it suspended like an exclamation mark. It made me flinch, but I tried to hide it. Any show of weakness would be fatal at this point.

"If you loved me, you'd do it. I'd do it for you." I rested my elbows on the table, looked up at him. He stared right at me, a small smirk playing around his lips.

"Have you any conceivable idea of what you're asking me?" I said.

"Of course I have, it's what I want. You wouldn't deny me, would you?"

Who was I kidding? Of course I wouldn't. I couldn't deny him anything, never had, but that's not how the game was played. It was easy to say, "I don't know. I don't think you want it enough."

"How do you know how much I want it? You just don't care enough," he said. We'd got to this point already. I guess he really did want it.

"That's not true. Maybe." He grinned; it was wolfish, and he was handsome in a way I couldn't resist. What was a toe when it came to true love?

"That means yes. I love you." He bestowed on me a genuine smile now. He always got what he wanted, one way or another. He stood up and walked around the table, kissing me full on the mouth as he extracted the knife from the scarred wood.

In the days leading up to that first act I was fraught with anxiety, never knowing when it would happen or where or even if it would happen at all. The knife was as omnipresent as my jumping nerves. The sweet taste of excitement and desire coated my tongue. He was so casual, so calm, as if the conversation had never occurred, but I knew this demeanor was studied. I saw how he looked at me, massaging my feet as I lay on the couch feigning sleep. I saw the way his glance slid to the knife on the bedside table as he kissed my hip in the bedroom. Even in the street he sized me up, drawing and quartering me. He could wait forever; that was the part he liked best, while I was dizzy with lust and fear.

I almost didn't notice when it did happen. The afternoon was hot and sticky and my skin feverish as he carried me to the bedroom. I must have sensed something because I felt detached and watched dust motes dance in the sunlight streaming from the window as he undressed me. He moved down my body with care, his long fingers firm and his kiss soft on my skin. I watched him as he cupped my foot in his hand, inspecting it. And the other hand? The knife. I hadn't noticed it disappear from the bedside table. He held it up to the light, shining the reflection in my eyes, and then he brought it down. The knife slid through my skin easily and the pain had a slight delay. He placed my detached smallest toe between his teeth, showing it to me before popping it into his mouth and then swallowing. He kissed my forehead and stroked my hair. "I love you more than life itself." The blood was warm as it spread over the bed sheets. The metallic smell fixed in my mind as the sweetness of sacrifice.

I had thought that was the end of it. I had thought his appetite had been satisfied, that the incident was an aberration in our everyday lives. But every step I took reminded me of it, the physical pain a memento for just how much he had wanted me, and I longed to be so desired again. My days were bittersweet with longing and a throbbing where flesh used to be. I had underestimated him, of course. Who knew better than me that his hunger would never be slaked, that he would want more and more and I would cave in endlessly, as much for my own satisfaction as for the need to please him.

He paced up and down the room, shirtless and ranting, knife in his hand. His chest glistened with sweat. The late summer heat had not abated. I sat on the couch watching. I never could take my eyes off him. "But don't you see? It's the ultimate expression of love. I consumed part of you; you're inside me and I've never felt more alive. You've given me power. By giving up your flesh you have given yourself to me. We can't stop now. We can't. Why should we deny ourselves? We've found something, you and I. Something others could only dream of."

He stood in front of me and drew the knife across his ribs. The blood didn't pour as I expected; it oozed, dark and viscous. He grabbed me by the hair and pushed my face into the wound. "Drink it, drink it for me. We'll be bound forever."

It filled my mouth and nostrils, warm and tangy, and I was tasting him, his scent filling my senses. As I inspected my gore-covered face in the bathroom mirror I realized that I liked it. I liked it a lot.

⋙✦⋘

It was a month later when he came up behind me and nuzzled my neck. "Open your mouth and close your eyes."

"What?"

"Open your mouth and close your eyes." His voice was full of glee.

"No!"

"Oh, go on. I have a surprise for you. It'll be worth it."

"No!"

"You're no fun anymore." I sighed. I could feel his pout on my neck.

"Okay." I closed my eyes and opened my mouth. What was I expecting? I don't know. He put the object in my mouth. It was small and salty.

"Now swallow. I dare you." I never could resist a dare. Gagging, I swallowed, just to prove that I wasn't chicken. He grabbed me by the shoulders and turned me round. Blood was running down his neck, the red angry against his pale skin. I followed the flow of blood to its source: his earlobe was missing. "Now we're even," he chuckled as he stalked out of the room. "My turn next."

I should have been angry at the way he had treated me, the way I had fallen for a schoolyard trick, but I couldn't bring myself to feel it. I admired his deviousness, his deception. How could I not respect someone who could play me so well? He had me falling over myself to try to match him, to please him, to engage in the game. My insecurity spurred me on. Every bit of attention he bestowed on me made the days when he turned away worth it, and I was as addicted to him as ever. The stakes were now higher, but the game had not changed. It was endless and all-consuming, and I was as willingly trapped as ever.

⇒⇒⇒⇐⇐⇐

Nothing happened for a while. Summer ended and winter held its cold grasp for months. I knew that it wasn't over, but we had all the time in the world, and wounds to heal. We carried on our normal lives. Danced around each other, circling like mountain cats. We ate and slept, worked and fucked, all the while watching each other with obsessive awareness.

Valentine's Day brought rain, so the picnic we had planned was moved inside. The blanket was spread on the bed and we loaded it with grapes and strawberries and cherries, cakes and cream and chocolate. He popped open champagne and we gorged ourselves. We were normal, almost. I fed him cherries and he spat the stones at me. The cakes were squashed as we rolled on the bed. We were covered in food and each other. More than one craving had to be taken care of that day. We mauled each other for hours, my thirst for him almost painful and the timely releases a blessing.

Afterwards, we collapsed, exhausted. He leaned over me and circled my hip with his finger. He moved down to kiss me. I felt a short, sharp shock of pain as his teeth bit down on the tip of my tongue. He wrenched his head away, tearing at my flesh. "It's only the tip," he said after he had swallowed. I dabbed my bleeding mouth with a paper picnic napkin.

A small part of me wanted revenge after that. I sulked for a while. It bothered me that he would take without asking when he knew I would give him anything he wished. But it didn't last long. I couldn't hold a grudge, not with him. He would come in through the door and fix me with that grin of his and my face of thunder would melt in the glare of his sunniness. I knew it was my turn, but I knew it was he who was in control of it all. I didn't know how to broach the subject and I still didn't know whether I wanted to. Did I want this to carry on, or could I end it now? I dreamed a lot during the following months. My nighttimes filled with conflicts I couldn't solve, decisions I couldn't make.

My birthday was April 14th, and that morning there was a red box wrapped in red ribbon on the pillow next to me, where his head usually lay. A card lay on the top of it. I opened it first. Inside was a brief message: *Your turn...Happy Birthday.* I cast it to one side and tore open the box. Inside, nestled in blue satin was a gleaming silver scalpel, presented like the most precious of jewels. I picked it up, weighed it in my hand. It felt right. It was a delicate weapon I could wield. His shiny souvenir had made my decision for me. My nights of turmoil were over.

That night he lay on the bed, naked and glorious. "Your choice, birthday girl, a sliver of my fine flesh for your delectable palate." He winked at me. A thrill of power shuddered down my backbone and I took my time. I dragged my fingernails across his pale, hard body. I kissed and bit and licked. I pinched his skin between my thumb and middle finger, making a show of considering my choice. I settled on a section just above his hip bone. The scalpel glided as a knife through butter and I chewed this time. My disgust had vanished, replaced by a satisfaction I had never known before.

I wanted more of him, much more. We were matched in appetite now, but it was his turn and every chance he had to study a body part he stole. He took great pleasure in inspecting me. He reduced me to the sum of my parts, and each part was under consideration. He adored every inch of me, and I basked under his even closer scrutiny. I was wanted in return and these were the golden days.

For his birthday in June, he bought himself some bolt croppers. He used them to remove the index finger of my left hand. The best present I have ever given anyone. He gnawed on it as I brought out his birthday cake. He paused to blow out the candles.

The summer heat arrived and I noticed the change in him, as attuned as I was to every perceptible difference. He was ranting again and I listened, rapt to his raving:

"Don't you see I need more of you? I can't live without you. It is imperative that I consume you. I want you to be mine forever. It's the only way. No one will ever love you like I do. If you love me half as much, you would agree in a second."

I nodded in acquiescence. It wasn't a game anymore, and my turns were over. I had to prove I was worthy of his love. I always said I'd die for him, and it would have been churlish of me not to keep my promise. I counted the days as they were numbered and waited for him to make his ultimate move. He bought a hacksaw and an axe.

That day he was waiting behind the door as I walked in, hunting knife in hand. My first instinct was to run and he chased me into the bedroom, a morbid mockery of our life before. I thought I would sacrifice everything for him, but an instinct of self-preservation took over. I fought for my life, biting and scratching and kicking as he tried to pin me to the bed. He slashed at my arms with the knife, his eyes manic and feverish, the look I always gave in to until now. I wriggled and squirmed but his arms were everywhere, his grip biting at my skin. In a last desperate attempt, I slammed my forehead into his face. His nose burst like a water balloon. In that brief moment, I grabbed the bolt croppers from the bedside table and swung them at his head.

I knew with the sound that it was all over. He fell limp on the bed, still and beautiful.

I went and got the hacksaw. I considered the heart first, but what I really loved him for was his brain. I was hungry.

INFECTION

I have been friends with Lucy Parrington since we were small girls. We met at the market. She was up high in a carriage with her mother, a servant running back and forth to show Mrs. Parrington items so that none of their precious feet ever touched the ground. I was down below scrubbing in the dirt, helping my father, a cobbler, run his knife-sharpening machine that we took to the market every week to make a little extra money. Yet Lucy hung over the side of the carriage and addressed me directly. "What are you doing?" she asked. She looked like she was made from spun glass, her skin almost translucent. Her voice tinkled when she opened her mouth. Before I had time to answer, her mother chastised her for "not being ladylike," and drew her back into the carriage. Lucy threw me a mischievous grin that had me hooked for life. I ran after the carriage as they drove away, a hobgoblin with my messy hair and dirty, bare feet. When I couldn't run anymore, I watched them drive up the steep incline of Parrington Hill, their crooked family estate at the top, a monstrosity of a building that loomed over our town of Penworth.

What can I tell you about our friendship that shouldn't have been? A friendship that was entirely orchestrated by Lucy and followed to the letter by me. When, unbeknown to her mother, she would send the coachman, sworn to secrecy, to come and get me, with a change of clothing so I could play-act being from her class, being very careful never to speak in front of an adult and betray my station. The years of coaching she gave me so I could pass in society and have a separate, different life to the one I was born to. My mother and father, warmhearted, kind and yet somehow lacking due to the life I was exposed to, were happy for me to experience a life that they could never give me.

When we were small girls, how she would clutch me hotly and tell me I was the only one for her, the only friend she truly loved, and I, like a fool, worshipped and believed her completely. When we were older, young teens, she became my official patron, bringing me into the household to assist her. Not quite a maid, yet not quite family. A companion. Her mother did not approve, and neither did much of the town. All of society, high class and low, were not amenable to young girls acting above their station. The only one in favor was Horatio Parrington, Lucy's father, who adored his only daughter's contrariness, and so my moving up in the world was allowed to pass, despite the mutters of disdain from all corners.

All was well, until the appearance of Algernon Belovedly. What a ridiculous name! What a ridiculous man! He and Lucy had apparently been pals when they were children, but I could not remember him. Mrs. Parrington simply *adored* him, of course. He was handsome, in that affected way that men of his class are. I will never forget the first time I laid eyes on him, and my sheer astonishment at the change in Lucy's demeanor. He was announced after dinner. We were in the drawing room. Mr. Parrington had already retired to his study to drink and smoke cigars, so the lady of the house received Belovedly's card on a silver tray. Mrs. Parrington could not contain her excitement. She giggled like a schoolgirl and her voice went up several octaves. "Let him in, let him in," she squeak-barked to the maid.

"Who is it, Mama?" said Lucy, already bored. But Mrs. Parrington paid no attention to her daughter as Algernon entered the room. He paused in the doorway for maximum effect, the gaslights shining on his glossy hair. Mrs. Parrington rushed towards him like a rustling little tugboat. He kissed her hand without taking his eyes off Lucy. She feigned disinterest, but I saw the way her feet pointed directly towards him.

"And who is this enchanting creature?" Belovedly said, in his ridiculous, overly refined voice. As if he didn't know.

"My daughter, Lucy." Mrs. Parrington's chest puffed up like she was a taxidermied grouse. Lucy deigned to extend her hand to his lips, but I could see the smirk that she hid from him.

Of course, Algernon courted Lucy aggressively, and who could blame him? She was the loveliest girl around, and her father's money was lovelier still. He knew he had to keep himself on the topmost of Lucy's (and her mother's) mind. After all, there was no shortage of rivals when it came to the hand of Penworth's finest asset.

It upset me to share Lucy's attentions, but to be fair, Algernon was kind to me and, at least at first, included me in their activities. A tactic, I am sure, to get me onside and strengthen his suit. He took us on carriage rides through the park, nights at the opera, strolls along the promenade. Each night afterwards, Lucy and I would sit on our beds, combing out our hair and giggling about how silly he was, how effete, and Lucy would swear that there was no way that she would marry him, that she would not marry anyone. She would inherit her father's estate and we would grow to be old spinsters together, our old bodies to be as crooked and twisted as the house we resided in. I swore I belonged to her and this house forever.

That winter was a cold one, and iron-gray ice encased the roads and pathways. There was a chill in the air that could not be dispelled by a roaring fire. We holed up in the crooked manse, paring down our social calendar. Algernon was a constant visitor and more than once found himself happily stuck at the Parringtons', the weather too frightful to venture to his lodgings. It was around this time I began to sense Lucy pulling away from me. She didn't join in when I disparaged Algernon after a night of whist. They began to sit together, giggling and whispering about things I could not hear. Their heads bent together as Mrs. Parrington looked on approvingly. I don't remember Mr. Parrington being around at this time. He was often away on business. It was also around this time that Lucy began to cough. They were little, delicate coughs at first, a clearing of the throat here or there, nothing to be worried about. Mrs. Parrington got the maid to make Lucy a hot toddy of boiled water and honey, lemon and a drop of whisky to soothe the throat.

When did it all start to go wrong? How do I pull at the threads and see when it started? I don't think it matters now, no matter how much

I obsess about it. One night that winter, Lucy sat down on the bed and looked at me sadly. "How long is it since you visited your parents?" Something about her question put me on edge. I felt wary, like a feral thing sensing danger. I could not be pulled away from her, from this house.

"It was the summer," I replied.

"Don't you miss them?" she said.

"No," I replied, strange, unwanted tears welling in my eyes. "I have you. And my parents are very content with the situation as long as I am happy and safe." It was true. I had long since felt an estrangement between my parents and me, owing to my strange place in Penworth society, but it was not an unhappy or painful one. My parents loved me and were happy to have their daughter kept.

"Yes, you have me," said Lucy, "but family is family. You should pay them a visit."

"But you are my family!" I blurted out, loudly, those threatened tears free flowing now. Lucy tried to console me, but was consumed by a coughing fit so violent that I had to get the maid to administer the special tincture that the doctor had prescribed for Lucy's worsening malady. It contained laudanum, and as such, Lucy fell into a deep sleep. As I watched her slumber, I thought I had never seen her looking so beautiful. Her skin so pale it was transparent, her cheeks flushed and her lips rosy. I knew that under her eyelids, as she slept dreamlessly, her eyes would be sparkling like some supernatural nymph's. I lay down beside her and wrapped my arm around her diminishing waist.

Lucy never mentioned it again, but I did overhear a heated exchange between the Parringtons. I assumed it was about me. I heard voices coming from Mr. Parrington's study, so I stole up to the slightly ajar door to listen. Mrs. Parrington was shrill, as usual. "The girl does not belong here," she said. "What will she do? Go with them? She can't stay here. She must go back to the bottom of the hill."

Then Horatio's booming baritone: "You are talking about a young woman. I will not allow our daughter to pick someone up and then drop them like a doll. Shame on you, Lucretia. I thought you better bred than that." I imagined Mrs. Parrington turning pink at his slight, but who were "them" and where were they going? I stalked away so they would not know I was listening.

Soon it became apparent what they were referring to, and I saw clearly now what I had not wished to see, that I had purposely blinded myself to what I didn't want to know. We were all summoned to the main dining room: members of the household, guests, and staff alike. We stood crowded in one end of the room. Mr. and Mrs. Parrington entered first through the doors at the other end, the dark wood of the table an ocean between us. They were followed by Lucy and Algernon, arm in arm. Mr. Parrington made the announcement but, of course, Mrs. Parrington kept butting in.

"Mrs. Parrington and I are delighted to announce..."

"Over the moon," twittered Lucretia.

"The formal engagement of our beloved only daughter..."

"Much beloved daughter."

Mr. Parrington patted his wife's arm, to shut her up, I hoped. "To Mr. Algernon Belovedly."

Mrs. Parrington squeaked in delight. Her husband smiled at her, but no more or less broadly than usual. Algernon and his wife-to-be, my Lucy, looked longingly at each other. I knew Lucy well enough to know that her love was at least partially staged. Not enough to comfort me, though. I began to swoon and the room began to spin. The housekeeper, a woman who I had previously thought cold and disdainful towards me, held my arms to steady me and told me it was going to be all right. But it wasn't me who fainted; it was Lucy. She slumped to the floor, cracking her temple on the hearth. She was carried to her bed and nothing more was said about her unfortunate fall.

From here on, the household was a whirlwind of preparation. Not only for the Christmas dinner in which the engagement would be formally announced to society, but for the wedding itself, which would happen in spring. But another whirlwind was taking place throughout the house, one that spun underneath the veneer of happiness, one that was shadowy and whispered. It was a whirlwind of doctor's visits and calls for the specialists and surgeon consultants, suggestions of sanatoriums and much wringing of hands. I was removed from most of it, haunting the house that I had once called home, unneeded and unwanted. Lucy and I still shared a bed, increasingly her sick bed. In the middle of the night she would cry that she didn't want to die. I pretended that I was asleep.

It was then I began a habit, a dark, shameful habit that I would admit to no one else. It was no secret to me that I coveted Lucy's beauty and station. It was an ache that I had nursed ever since first seeing her as a child, leaning over that carriage, but it was something I could never do anything about until now. I had offered my soul to whoever was listening to acquire it. It was clear to me that Lucy's illness was accentuating her beauty, if that was even possible. Let us be frank with one another: we all knew what it was, but we were not saying it out loud. Her mother and father, me, the servants, even ridiculous Algernon, knew what ailed our Lucy. If we didn't say it, it didn't exist. If we didn't acknowledge it, then it wouldn't proceed to its foregone conclusion.

But of course, she would cough, cough, cough and soon she was hiding handkerchiefs all over the house, shameful little parcels that she would stuff under cushions, in drawers, between the mattress and bedframe, in pockets and shoes. When unraveled, each would reveal the tell-tale sign of bloody sputum. What did I do? Each one I stole away, and secretly licked the mess that she made. Disgusting? Yes. Dangerous? That too. But what did it matter? I was to lose Lucy. My life was nothing without her, and here I could end with a shadow of her beauty. Her contamination would give me the pinched cheeks and wan complexion, the feverish eyes and dark red lips. For a short while I could be admired and nevermore could someone sniff at my pretensions of class. Consumption would prove my gentility forever. The Parringtons sent the maid to the market to buy more linen, assuming it was Lucy who was discarding them.

Christmas came and went, the new year passed into being, and I continued my clandestine activities. Lucy became incandescent with sickness. Her beauty now was unsurpassed and it moved even me to see how this affected Algernon. He was at once dazzled by her magnificence and poleaxed with grief at the truth. Lucretia showed a talent for denial that I couldn't help but admire. The only member of the house that would take any note of me was Mr. Parrington. He asked how I was and looked kindly upon me. And yet, I showed no signs of illness, no matter how much infected material I consumed.

The wedding was moved forward to February. The official line was that the bride wanted to marry on Valentine's Day. Of course, the truth was much darker. No one knew if Lucy would last until spring. She wished to be married, and the Parringtons' money made every change possible.

How can one describe the day a best friend and confidante gets married? The mixture of joy and pain I felt! Lucy, looking lovelier than ever, yet moving painfully slowly down the aisle of the local church, leaning heavily on her father's arm. Her, I had to admit, handsome husband-to-be waiting for her, his face a mixture of agony and ecstasy. I watched it all from the front pew (something Horatio had insisted upon after Lucretia refused to allow me to be maid of honor). This was when I would lose my Lucy, but to who? Algernon or death?

Neither, immediately, as it would turn out. Due to Lucy's fragile condition, Algernon made the unusual step of moving in to the in-laws' home rather than take his bride away. The Parringtons gave them a suite in another part of the house, so I kept Lucy's room.

Those little linen parcels that had become so essential to my routine were harder to come by, but still I sought them out and, curiously, still did not get sick. Lucy hung on to life, barely. She was now bedridden, and I was afforded a visit once a day, thanks to

Algernon, who insisted on it. My feelings for him softened. It was clear that his grief was as deep as my own. Lucy did not say much. When she was awake, she was wracked by coughs that exhausted her into sleep. Occasionally, there were quiet times when she would stare at me mutely, her eyes huge and her cheeks sunken. I would wait until her eyes closed, then gather up the material she had choked into and run to my own quarters.

Yet Lucy was not the first to die. Lucretia went first. The great Mrs. Parrington, sturdy and robust, who succumbed to the sickness and passed away within a month. Her bustling, irritating presence was missed in the house. I took over running the home at Horatio's request. He, visibly diminished by the loss, kept to his study. I was lucky that the staff accepted my leadership, but we lost a few who were too afraid of illness to stay. Thus, I was the lady of the house, in a fashion. Was this not what I wanted? Some might think it a hollow victory, but there was satisfaction in it. But when I looked in the mirror I still saw myself, the dirty little girl from the marketplace.

Do I continue to pretend that what happened between Algernon and me happened after Lucy passed? I suppose not. What use is it now? She lingered longer than anyone would have guessed. Past her original wedding date, throughout the summer and into the fall. All Algernon and I could do was sit and wait for her to fail. After a particularly bad night, he stopped me in the hall and grabbed my wrist.

"Why does she linger so?" he said, his handsome eyes full of sorrow.

I shrugged. "I don't know."

"Do we need to tell her to go?"

"Maybe," I said. His shoulders began to shake as he tried to stop weeping. I don't know what came over me. Some compassion for the man I had previously held nothing but derision for? I enfolded him in an embrace and he sobbed into my shoulder. When his tears had subsided, he looked at me and we kissed awkwardly. I heard Horatio coughing in another part of the house and wondered if he would be next.

I was still so healthy, it disgusted me. I managed the house with ease, even as we lost the majority of the staff to illness or abandonment. The inhabitants of the house no longer noticed if everything wasn't as clean as it was, and the cook stayed under the proviso that she would leave food in the drawing room and the rest of us would not enter the kitchen. I presume that the rest of Penworth knew of our situation, but kept their distance. My mother and father tried to help once, but I sent them away for their own good. I was taking all of Lucy's handkerchiefs and had consumed Mrs. Parrington's infection during her short illness. Still, I was untouchable.

I told Lucy to go as I held her pillow over her face. She was so weak by then, it didn't take much, a merciful act for the one I loved the most. She was more beautiful in death than I could ever reach. Seeing Algernon fawn over her body hurt, but it was Horatio's reaction that harrowed me the most. To see such a man be felled like a giant oak by grief was humbling.

He was now the one who coughed and coughed, and I stole away his linens as I had done the rest. Ever the practical man, Horatio wanted me to be taken care of. He signed everything over to Algernon and consented for us to be married. The housekeeper found a reverend that would risk entering the house. It was a sombre affair, one rooted more in mourning than in love. I had not considered a wedding for myself. When my husband made love to me, I pretended it was Lucy back from the grave.

Horatio was gone soon after the wedding, and by that time Algernon was already coughing. I continued to kiss him deeply, despite his protests, and still nothing. Was I cursed? We heard from those who were brave enough to visit that the sickness was racing through the village like wildfire. They told us that they blamed Parrington Hill. The sickness had started with the arrival of Algernon and the death of Lucy. There were rumors that Lucy roamed the village, even after death; that she stole children and breathed the sickness into them to spread to their kin. The stable boy told me that my parents were gone as he ran down the hill away from me. They all died around me: Lucy, the Parringtons, the cook and the housekeeper. I stood in the magnificent crooked house as my husband faded away. Now I was mistress to all I surveyed with no one to witness it: my love, Lucy, lost, and I never possessing her beauty as mine.

How long have I been here? Long, too long. I can't look at my image in the mirror anymore. The house has ruined around me and Penworth too. How is it possible I exist when there is no one to see me? If I started coughing now, how would I truly know with no one to hear it?

JANINE

She scratched her head, showing dark roots underneath her stiff blonde hair, and took a deep drag on a cigarette.

"Janine, you know you can't smoke in the bar anymore," shouted the bartender.

Janine extended her middle finger to him, her nail polish bright blue and chipped. "Fuck off, Bob, we all know I'm pretty much your only customer." She turned her gaze to Amanda. Her pale gray eyes were opioid-pinned. "So what do you want to know?"

Her partner had warned Amanda against meeting Janine. "She's crazy, you know, not crazy-but-town-treasure crazy, dangerous crazy. Into all kinds of shit: drugs, illegal stuff. Plus, there was that stuff with her boyfriend way back." When she'd asked them to elaborate, they shook their head. "Stay away from her. She's a trainwreck." Of course, Amanda wasn't going to listen.

"I'll think about it," she said, knowing full well that she was going to call Janine the next morning. Her name was in the phone book, and she'd heard mutters around town about Janine blaming little blue devils for something that had happened long ago. Amanda needed a scoop that would turn her boss's head at the paper. Something different. Something that might save her job. Janine's voice was slurry from sleep or something else when she answered the phone, but she agreed to meet on the condition that they met in the local bar and that Amanda was buying.

It was 11 a.m. in the knotty pine cocoon of the Draft Pub, Amanda nursing a coffee and Janine making her way through several strong white ciders at an alarming speed. It was clear that Janine had been attractive once, but time and lifestyle had ravaged her looks. There were dark circles under her creased eyes, her cheeks were red with old acne scars and thread veins, and her lips were dry and chapped. A deep worry line bisected her forehead.

They didn't make small talk. Amanda was feeling too desperate to dance around. "I want to know about your experience with the blue devils."

Janine guffawed, showing rotted teeth at the back of her mouth. "Jesus Christ, are you telling me you believe me?"

Amanda shrugged. "I don't know. Tell me what happened."

Janine's vacant eyes got teary. "No one fucking believes me, you know." She chewed at her nails. "We were in love. We were young, but we loved each other. Everyone who talks around town always forgets that part. Makes it easier for them to live with the things they say about me." Janine used her finger to swipe a tear from under her eye without smudging her mascara. "I was a freshman when we got together. I was fourteen years old. I know it's hard to believe, but I was the prettiest girl in school." She laughed bitterly. "Didn't make me popular, though, just the opposite. What did a trashy girl from the trailer park have any business being pretty? Most of the boys tried it with me, and some of the men. So the girls hated me. Didn't matter that I didn't do nothing. They called me a slut anyhow, as did the boys when I turned them down. With a mom that was known to do tricks on occasion and a dad who was a drunk, how did they expect me to turn out?"

"But you were just a kid," said Amanda.

"That doesn't matter in a small place like this." Amanda waved at the barman to get Janine another drink and ordered herself a beer. So what if it was noon? She could always leave the car and walk home. Out of everyone she had ever interviewed, Janine seemed the loneliest.

"Dane was different, though. He didn't try to get into my pants first chance he got, and he was kind to me. Told the other kids to leave me alone when I got on the bus. He was good-looking, tall and not too skinny, with dark brown hair and the bluest eyes...and rich. Whoo boy, the look on my momma's face when I brought him home. I'm sure his mom wasn't pleased about him hooking up with the likes of me, but she never showed it. She was always so sweet to me...of course, she never spoke to me again after that night. Never spoke to anyone. She left town soon after. I heard she was a shut-in." Janine sighed heavily. "Are you sure you want to hear the rest? I mean, you won't believe me."

Amanda reached across the table and touched Janine's hand. It was far colder than it should have been. "You can tell me, Janine," she said.

"We'd been together for four years at that point. People talk like it was a one-night thing, but we'd been together longer than some people's marriages, you know? Even if we were young. I mean, we'd fooled around, what teenagers wouldn't in four years? But I was a virgin still, and I'm assuming he was. It was 1989. I was waiting for prom. I still had ridiculous romantic notions back then. I don't think I thought he would ever marry me, even though he always said he would. I figured he'd go to college, find some rich girl, and that'd be that. People like Dane's family stick to their own. Hell, so do we. The amount of guys I've dated since who are just like my daddy." She gave out a harsh bark of a laugh. "I knew this even back then. I wanted him to be my first before I slunk back to the level I was supposed to be at. We decided on prom. They still called it the Blueberry Ball back then, isn't that a hoot? With the Blueberry King and Queen, but I'm getting ahead of myself."

Bob brought the drinks to the table. When Amanda looked up at him, he eyerolled towards Janine.

"My mom got me a dress. I have no idea how or what she had to do to get me one, but she did it. I think managing to get Dane and going to the prom are the only things my mom has ever been proud of me for. She was so fucking happy to give me that dress. It was a real eighties number: it was white, puffy sleeves and lots of lace, you remember those? You're probably too young, but man, it was a great dress. I walked down those damned trailer steps like a princess. You should have seen Dane's face when he saw me. Those blue eyes of his shined when he pinned the corsage to my shoulder. I know it was love that was there. No man has ever looked at me like that before or since.

I only got it once, with Dane. I suppose I was lucky to get that, right?" Janine drained the rest of her drink, gulping down the alcohol as if her life depended on it.

"Want another?" said Amanda, despite her misgivings that she might be giving Janine too much to drink. But Janine nodded and Bob continued to serve them, so what the hell?

"Fuck it," said Janine, "I'll just show you. It's not like I can show anyone else." She took an old photo out of her worn purse. It was old and creased, blurry at the edges from continued greasy fingerprints. It had that haziness to it that photos from the eighties had. Janine flattened it out on the table and slid it over to Amanda.

There they were, stood on the steps of a broken-down trailer. It was a little surreal to see the younger, really quite lovely version of Janine, and *Christ*, she looked so happy. Beaming in that very eighties prom dress and big, big hair. It made Amanda's heart ache to see the difference between Janine then and the Janine sat in front of her. When did the light go out of her eyes? Was it that night? There was Dane, a young kid, just about to be a man. Good-looking, yes, but even in the photograph, it was clear he had that easy confidence that came with never really having to struggle, something Janine probably never knew. Where was he now?

Janine grabbed the photo and jammed it back in her bag. "I always carry it with me," she said, "but I can't look at it too long." She shook her head as if dispelling a memory. "What was your prom like?"

Amanda shrugged. "It was, you know, the usual."

"I bet you were the prom queen, with looks like yours."

Amanda reddened. She had been the prom queen. "Enough about me." She tried to hide the impatience in her voice. "Tell me what happened, Janine."

"My prom night was magical. I know it sounds corny, but it's true. The gym looked amazing. I didn't even mind the stupid blueberry theme. All of the walls were draped with that blue see-through material that seems to float. I almost didn't recognize the place. Not that I spent much time in the gym, usually." She snorted at her own joke. "The band was local, but a good one. They played all the hits, and me and Dane danced all night. Had our pictures taken. Although I never did collect them...what with everything. I wish I had them now. I was the prom queen, too." She grinned. Amanda was about to interrupt her, to say she'd never said. "I could tell by the way you looked embarrassed and proud at the same time. Yeah, I was the fucking Blueberry Queen. Of course, there was no question that Dane would be the Blueberry King, but he had gone around and convinced everyone to vote for me. I didn't hear the last of that after." Janine didn't hide the bitterness from her voice. "But I'm getting ahead of myself. Standing on that stage, wearing that silly crown with the plastic blueberries on it...for the first time, I felt part of things. Like I wasn't destined to fail, that Dane and I would be together forever, that I could maybe escape. Sheesh, what a dummy I was."

Janine lit another cigarette. Bob tutted in the background. Amanda noticed Janine's hands were shaking. "Are you okay?" she said. Janine managed a shaky smile.

"Oh, sure," she said. "It's just been a while since I told this story." She didn't look okay. She took a deep breath. "Anyway, we danced the last dance together. I can't remember the song now. I know I loved it. Maybe I've just blocked that part out. I wish I could block the rest of it. But at that point, it was the best night of my life. But you want to know what happened next, right?"

Amanda nodded.

"I'm going to need something stronger to drink. Whiskey."

Amanda waved Bob over. "Two whiskeys, please. Make them doubles." When the drinks arrived at the table, Janine threw hers back.

"Okay," she said. Amanda sipped her drink and sat back in the chair.

"You didn't grow up here?" Janine said. Amanda shook her head. "Well, back then, if you wanted to park, you know what I mean, you drove to the woods behind the high school. I don't know if they still do it now. There's always been tons of scary stories about the woods, but you know teenagers: they're horny and they think they're invincible. I imagine they're just the same now.

"I've seen on TV that kids these days book hotel rooms for after prom, but it just wasn't done then around here, even if you did have the money like Dane. Besides, there's nowhere here that you can go and stay anonymously. *Everywhere* is owned by someone you know, or back then, someone your parents knew. Not that my parents gave much of a shit, but Dane's family had a reputation to uphold.

"We left the prom as soon as it ended and drove into the woods to the very end of the dirt track, deep in there, the very best spot. I guess it was only fitting that the Blueberry King and Queen got it, right?" Janine laughed, but it was hollow. Amanda could tell she was stalling. Was it all a ruse to get more drinks out of her? No, there was no disguising the pain in Janine's face. "We began to fool around. Moved into the backseat. I'm going to assume that you know what I'm talking about. A looker like you doesn't get to your age without fooling around in a car, and if you haven't, well, then I'm sorry. We were inexperienced and clumsy, but at that age it doesn't matter. I was just so glad that we had finally done it, and that he was my first. He looked so lovely afterwards in the backseat of that car, both of us so young, half-dressed and glowing. I still remember the smell of him after all these years, that earthy fresh sweat smell and feeling the warmth of his neck as I pressed my face against it. I think about that feeling a lot, you know? It was the last time I was happy.

"We sat in the back, holding each other. He was talking and talking. Nerves, I suppose. I wasn't really listening. He was talking about having to go to college, but he would send for me, and maybe I could find a way to go to college too, and that we could get married. It was crazy talk, of course. None of that would happen, but I loved him for saying it. He was halfway through describing his plans of getting a part-time job and apartment off-campus when there was a huge bang against the side of the car, and then a screech as if something was scratching the side of the car with something metallic. We both damn near jumped out of our skins, but then we're laughing, because clearly it's some other kids messing around, right?

"We both got dressed quickly. I watched Dane pull up his pants and thought about how I couldn't wait to get him back out of them. We got out, and there are these huge gouges in the paint down the side of the car and Dane mutters 'motherfuckers,' because everyone's heard of that urban legend, the one with the guy with the hook, and of course, it's kids from our school pranking us. Maybe they were upset because I got to be Blueberry Queen, who the fuck knows, but what's weird is these gouges, they aren't like a hook mark, more like a claw has scratched down the side, and there's a dent near the door handle, which must have been the bang we heard. Dane shouted into the woods, 'Who's there? You'll pay for the body work, you fuckers,' but there's nothing. I expected to hear laughing or them running away or something, but it was quiet. All I remember hearing is Dane breathing, and the evening air giving me goosebumps on my bare skin.

"Then we hear a chittering. You know, like cats make when they want to get at something, but louder. I had a cat once that ate bugs...used to hunt them down in the trailer. He used to make that noise when there was a moth or spider he couldn't reach." Janine made the noise, her teeth chattering. Amanda would have laughed, but Janine's face had gone gray and she was staring off into the distance as if she couldn't see Amanda at all.

"Dane looked around at me and shrugged. I guess we still thought it was kids at that point. It was the last time we really looked at each other. There was a rustling in the trees. 'Get in the car, Janine,' Dane said, and I did what he told me. He always protected me. I watched him walk towards where the noise came from, but then these *things* started coming out of the woods."

"What things, Janine?" Amanda said, but she knew what was coming.

"There were five of them," said Janine. "They were—fuck, they were little things about three feet tall? They came up to here on Dane." She placed her hand at her stomach. "And Dane was near six foot, but there were five of them." She was fully crying now and wiped away tears with the flat of her hand. "They were blue. Their skin was blue and thin, like you could see the veins through it. They had these little nubby horns on their heads, almost like baby deer have, but they weren't cute. No. Their eyes were dark red and shining, like aliens, and they had claws and these horrible sharp teeth, ragged and pointed and needle-like like those deep-sea fish you see on the Animal Channel.

"I never saw anything like those things. People around here call them the blue devils. All the crazy people, at least, but I never did go for that Jesus stuff. If I don't believe in that, how can I believe in devils? They came from the woods, and they weren't people but they weren't quite animals either. I don't know what the fuck they were. Maybe I'm crazier than a shithouse rat too.

"They walked towards him, almost like little kids coming up to a grown-up. Dane started backing up, stumbling a little on tree roots. He was shaking his head. He couldn't believe what he was seeing either. He started to turn to run, I suppose, but that's when they pounced on him. They could jump so high, for little things. They scrambled all over him, grabbing him with their claws and using their weight to pull him down. If there was one or two he could have easily shook them off, but there were five. I could see the blood starting to run where they stuck their claws in him. In seconds, he fell to the ground and they dragged him into the woods. It happened so quickly. Like he was never there at all."

"What did you do?" asked Amanda.

Janine twitched as if coming out of a dream. She looked directly into Amanda's eyes. "I ran. I never learned how to drive, so I got out of the car and ran back to town, barefoot. Tore my feet up real good. I'm no-good trash like the rest of my family. A coward. I should have gone into the woods. Tried to save the man I loved...or at least died with him."

"No. You did the right thing."

"Did I? I don't think so. I'm as guilty as they say I am. They all think it was me that did it, and in a way I let it happen. I should have tried to save him." Janine rubbed both hands over her face, smearing her mascara. She lit another cigarette. Amanda waited until she was ready to speak again.

"I went to the police. I told them that something had dragged Dane into the woods. I didn't tell them it was little fucking blue creatures. I couldn't believe it myself. Thought I was having some kind of breakdown. They didn't believe me anyway. Thought I was making up stories for being out late after prom. They didn't go looking for him until his mother called the next morning when he didn't come home."

"Did they find him?"

"He was 20 feet away from his car. Well, what was left of his body was. The police came over and dragged my ass out of bed the next day. I was still wearing my prom dress. I hadn't slept. I lay there all night, reliving those things dragging him into the woods. I thought they were coming for me. I thought I heard them scratching outside the trailer.

"The cops showed me photographs of the scene, pictures of Dane's body. I didn't have no lawyer or even a parent with me. They tried to get me to confess. To say I'd done it, but how could I have? They'd scratched and bitten him all over. His hands and feet were chewed, almost gone. They'd taken, they'd..." Janine began gulping, as if she couldn't get any air. "Clawed out his eyes. His beautiful blue eyes."

Janine stubbed out her cigarette and stood up suddenly, knocking over the drinks on the table. "I have to go," she muttered, and ran out into the street.

Amanda stood up, her skirt drenched in booze. She shouted, "Janine, wait." But when she got to the window she could see Janine running, as if she was being chased, up the middle of the road. Passersby stopped to point and whisper.

Amanda had expected to see Janine around town, or at least hear about her. Now that she had heard her story, what worried Amanda wasn't the truth of it or not, but what it cost Janine to tell her. When she didn't answer her calls, Amanda went back to the bar to ask Bob if he had seen Janine.

"Nope, gone to rehab in the city, I heard," said Bob. "About time, too. Her whole life wasted. She isn't a bad person, you know."

"I never slept properly, you know, after that night. That's why I took so many pills." Janine sat on a plastic chair in the visitors' room, a sparse area with clinical green walls and a threadbare carpet. Amanda had found her in a clinic in Portland. She was surprised that Janine had agreed to see her. "No one else has visited," said Janine, "and I wanted to finish telling you." Janine looked worse than before, despite her claims that she was getting better. She was near skeletal now, with no makeup to hide behind and scratches up and down her arms. "I didn't tell you the whole truth about why I was so upset with myself for not going in the woods. I should have tried to save Dane, that was true, but here's the thing: they should have taken me too. That night, I really could hear them outside and every night, I would hear them, scratching the outside of our trailer. Waiting for me to come outside, but I never did. I took the booze and the pills and the powder and did what I could not to hear them. But I *have* to hear them. I know that now. I have to stop hiding. I have to let them in. My life ended that night, just like Dane's did. It's just taken me this long to realize it." Amanda urged Janine to talk to her doctors, but she refused. She just smiled sadly at Amanda when visiting time was over. Amanda tried to talk to someone on the way out, but the receptionist said they couldn't discuss a patient with someone who wasn't a family member.

A week later, Janine was dead. Suicide. It was all over the local news. She'd been found in the woods, so it was public knowledge. No one knew how she'd gotten out of rehab. Slashed her wrists so deep her hands were almost detached. But before she'd done that, she'd tried to scratch out her own eyes. Amanda went to Janine's parents' to give her condolences. They wouldn't open the door. Deep gouges ran the circumference of their trailer. Amanda trashed her story and got out of town.

SURVIVING MY PARENTS

"**S**he wants to have Dad stuffed."

My sister, Clarrie, was in Spain. At the age of thirty-five, she had decided to quit her job and travel Europe with Jen, a "friend" from work. Despite being across the Atlantic, she still had a firmer grasp on family affairs than I did. I stayed away on purpose.

"I'm sorry, Clarrie, the line is pretty bad. For a minute I thought you said that Mom wanted to stuff Dad." I watched Poppy, my King Charles spaniel, through the kitchen window. She was following a beetle with her nose, her long golden ears dragging on the floor. She was half-scared of the beetle, I could tell, but was pretending to be brave. She gave it a tentative lick.

"That's exactly what I said, Ralph. She wants to stuff him. Taxi-whatsit. Like those jackalopes in Mangy Moose."

"But he's not dead yet."

"I know that, Ralph. I suspect she'll wait."

"What are we going to do?"

"Oh-ho," she chuckled. "It's your turn. You can go down there."

I cringed. "How is your...Jen?"

"She's fine. We're both wonderful, actually."

A few days later, I found myself on a tiny plane bumping onto the asphalt of Orlando airport. I hired a car there. I didn't trust my mother's driving, and my father's failing eyesight had stopped him from driving long ago. I made my way to their small ranch in the suburbs, and on the way I rehearsed what I was going to say. The air conditioner didn't work in the rental car. Sweat poured from my head, making my bald patch more noticeable. Dark brown stains bloomed under the arms of my sports coat. I wished I was home with Poppy. I'd left her with my neighbor, Rochelle, but I knew Poppy would miss me. Rochelle meant well, but she was too loud and smelled of nail polish.

I rarely had time off work, so requesting some vacation time was no problem. It bothered me to leave it to others. I'm an auditor for a well-known insurance company. I check facts and make sure all the numbers add up. You can't argue with spreadsheets. They don't have tantrums and not speak to you for weeks, they don't say embarrassing things to your friends, and they don't run off with women called Jen.

I pulled the car into my parents' driveway. I saw that my mother hadn't gotten rid of the plastic flowers next to the door like I asked her to. I rang the doorbell.

"We're 'round the back, come 'round," my father shouted. I could have been anyone: an axe murderer, a rapist—one of those gangs you read about. I told them this as I walked through the gate, only to be confronted by the sight of my mother's ample behind, clad only in the tiniest of bikinis. My hands flew up to my face for protection. She turned around.

"I shouldn't think so, Ralph, why on earth would they ring the doorbell?" I began to peer through my fingers. "And why are you flinching, have you got something in your eye?" The only other items of clothing she wore were bright pink gardening gloves. My father was standing by the barbeque. He waved a spatula at me.

"Can I interest you in a wiener?" He wore a chef's apron over Bermuda shorts that bore the legend *King of the Grill*. Neither of them looked shocked to see me.

My mother walked over to me and undid the top button of my shirt. I wrestled her fingers away and re-buttoned it. She rolled her eyes. "I knew as soon as I had spoken to Clarabelle that our news would induce a visit, and seeing as how she's gallivanting around Europe, I figured it would be you. Come on, let's get you settled in." She bustled through the back door and into the house. "We're not changing our minds," she shouted from within. I looked around at my father. He smiled and poked the grill.

I followed her into the guest room, stepping over what looked like grass skirts strewn on the floor. A tiki statue in the corner gave me a baleful look.

"We had a luau last week," she said. She took my suitcase from me and threw it on the bed. "How long are you staying?" she asked.

"For as long as it takes for you both to see sense."

"You're going to be here a long while, then. You're wasting your time. You should have stayed in Maine."

"Mother, this is ridiculous..."

"No. It's what we both want." She looked up at me, chin thrust outwards, her hands on her hips. "It's not up for discussion." Her hot pink lipstick was seeping into the tan wrinkles around her puckered lips.

"But, Mother," I held the palms of my hands towards her, "you're talking about human taxidermy."

She held up a finger pointing it to the sky. "I'm talking about creative post-life decisions."

I could hear the tone of my voice climbing higher and higher. "You're talking about stuffing my father."

She harrumphed. "Well, if you're going to be negative."

"How about cocktails?" I turned around to my father, who had materialized behind me. He passed me a coconut with a straw poking out of the top. I wasn't sure how many times I had told my father that I didn't drink, but I took it anyway.

That night I rang Rochelle. "It looks like I might have to stay awhile, could be the rest of the week."

"No worries, Ralphie, we're getting along famously."

I cringed; I hated being called Ralphie.

"We're just settling down to watch the soaps and eating chocolate."

"Don't give Poppy chocolate."

"She's just had a little—it didn't hurt you, girl, did it?"

I could hear her making kissy noises. A vein in my forehead throbbed. "Well don't give her any more."

"I won't, Ralphie."

"Could you," I paused. "Could you put her on?" Poppy snuffled down the line. I felt sick for home, to be in my own bed, laid reading, Poppy at the side of me. "You be a good girl now for Rochelle, okay? Daddy'll be home soon. Now put Rochelle back on. There's a good girl."

Rochelle snapped gum in my ear. "Don't you worry, Ralphie, us girls'll be fine. You do what you have to do." As I put the phone back on the receiver, I could hear *Wheel of Fortune* on too loud in her living room.

The next morning, Mother had me pushing the cart through the local grocery store. I avoided the subject while she went through a shopping list that seemed never-ending. For every item, she consulted a huge pile of coupons to see if she could make a saving.

"We have to get root beer for your father." I passed her his usual brand. "Not that one, the diet—he'll never know." She gave me a wink. "I decant it into a regular bottle." I rolled my eyes at her. She pretended not to notice. She scanned the shelves with expert precision, always taking the third from the front of every product. "The first has probably been tampered with," she said, "the second has been thumbed by everyone who's thinking about buying it." She nodded to herself. "And the one at the back is where the boy who stacks the shelves put the one that he dropped." She picked up the third tin of tuna off the shelf. "You have to think, Ralph. Learn to read people. Like Robert says, most people are sheep in their behaviors. If you're smart you can do things your own way." I didn't like the sound of this. My mother, of all people, didn't need encouraging to do things her own way.

"Who's Robert, Mother?"

She harrumphed again and waddled down to the frozen food section.

⟫⟪

I found the brochure later that day. It was a nauseating shade of mid-purple. Not light enough to be lilac or lavender, yet not dark enough to be truly purple. The lettering was a yellow color, probably called "gold" in the printer's catalog. I read the highlights to Clarrie while my parents were at the Hubermans' for their Wednesday night euchre.

"Here on the front," I read, "'After Alternatives: Your Ultimate Guide in Post-Life Options.'"

"Does it have a price list?" she said.

"I'm getting to that."

The more I read, the more I marveled at my mother being suckered into such an enterprise. We had our differences, but I would have never imagined my mother to have been caught up in something so tacky. The brochure avoided the words "death" or "dying," of course, and it made the afterlife seem like one of those all-expenses-paid cruise trips that the over-65's seem to spend all their kids' inheritance on.

"It says here that you have to speak to one of the consultants who will 'tailor your end-space plans just for you.'"

"End-space? Good lord."

"It's all very vague, Clarrie. There are different packages you can have. One makes allusions to the Egyptians. Another, I think, is being frozen. This one here, 'We Are Made of Stars,' seems to involve shooting up your 'particles' in a firework."

"Which is the 'be upholstered and sit in your favorite armchair for eternity' package?"

"Clarrie, what if she does it? What if she actually, somehow, goes through with it?"

"She won't, Ralph. I'm fairly sure it's not even possible. Or legal."

I turned the page.

"It costs $100,000."

The line went silent for a moment.

"You have to stop her."

⫸✦⫷

Later, after Clarrie had gone to sleep somewhere across the Atlantic, I turned to the back of the brochure that lay stranded in my lap. A tanned face with twinkling eyes and an insincere smile looked up at me: "Robert Hamilton, Director." I went to the den and cranked up my mother's ancient computer and started doing my homework.

I knew that all the regular arguments about common sense and ethics wouldn't sway my mother. I needed cold, hard facts. Practical reasons she couldn't argue with. At about two in the morning, when much to my disgust, my parents still hadn't come home, I hit gold— proof to my mother that this hare-brained scheme of hers wasn't feasible. I slept soundly after that, ready to confront her in the morning.

I waved a flag of print-outs at my mother at the breakfast table. My father was absent, which was unusual.

"You can't do it." I thumped them down next to her cereal, a muesli concoction that looked like dried twigs. She was dressed in a coral-colored bathrobe. She looked up at me and spoke with her mouth full.

"Can't do what?"

"That thing," I waved my hand at her in a winding motion, "to Dad. This is proof that that Robert guy is scamming you."

She squinted at the sheaf of papers. "What's it say? I haven't got my readers."

"It says that generally, human skin is too thin to withstand the taxidermy process well."

"Look, Ralph..."

"A view corroborated by Wild Ben of Ben's Taxidermy, who was kind enough to answer my email this morning."

"Ralph."

"Also, by the law of this state, a cadaver has to be embalmed if it is going to be viewed. Now, you have to agree, having my father sitting in the living room, post-life, is a 'viewing' situation."

"Yes, but..."

"And I'm fairly sure the fluids used in the embalming process are poisonous. You wouldn't want Dad leaking all over the couch."

"For God's sake," my mother shrieked at me. I stood there blinking. "I knew you would be like this. I am your mother. Don't tell me what I can and can't do." My mother, to my astonishment, had tears in her eyes. "We're not changing our minds." She fled the room.

She didn't return to the house for the rest of the day, but where she could have gone dressed only in her bathrobe, I could only guess. Her reaction had unnerved me. I felt uncomfortable, here in the house that she and Dad shared but I had never lived in. As I looked at the photos on the walls and in frames on every surface, I saw that my mother and father had built a life of their own quite separate from Clarrie and me. While we assumed to be making our own way in the world, as selfish children we didn't realize that our parents were building a life away from us, too. I felt like an intruder.

⟫⟫⟫⟪⟪⟪

I was packing my things when a shadow caught my eye. It was Dad, standing in the doorway. I had no idea how long he had been there.

"You leaving us?" That friendly tone never left his voice. I had never known him to shout, or sound angry, or annoyed even. I pouted a little.

"I'm fairly sure I've outstayed my welcome. Mother stormed out on me earlier."

"Well, you know your mother, a little hot-headed when it comes to something she's fixed her mind on." I tried to discern from his eyes what he thought of all this—how he could continue humoring her even when it came to desecrating his own remains.

"How can you let her do this?"

"Because I love her. Your mother can do whatever she wants when it comes to me."

"You'd be a laughing stock; a carnival exhibit."

"I expect by that point I won't care much."

"But what about your savings? She's spending it all on this."

My father smiled at me and sat down on the bed. He was creasing my best shirt.

"I'm dying, Ralphie."

I hate being called Ralphie wasn't the first thing I expected to run through my mind, but I guess you don't get to choose these things. I had a sense of the ground shifting underneath me, like I had just gotten off a fairground ride and hadn't gotten my balance back.

Taxidermy, state laws, even getting the better of my mother seemed to recede into the background at the prospect of losing the man who was the steadiest presence I had ever known. I looked up at my father. The expression in his green-gray eyes never wavered, and his unkempt eyebrows were making an attempt to connect with the wispy hair that remained on his head.

"Dad, can't they do something?"

"I have about three months at the most. Cancer. We didn't know how to tell you, or Clarabelle. We didn't want you to worry, and I didn't want a fuss—but well, you know your mother, she could cause a fuss in a convent." He grinned. "I know this must be tough on you, and I know that it really isn't fair on you or Clarrie." He put his blue-veined hand over mine and I fixed my gaze on the liver spots around his knuckles. "But I need the time I have left to be about me and your mother. I know what you think about her. I know she's irrational and bossy and irresponsible, but she's the greatest thing that ever happened to me. I know I'm supposed to say it's you kids, but I figure you're old enough to pay for your own therapy. She has always been and always will be the reason I was put here. So she can do anything—anything to my sorry old shell once I've gone. Anything to make herself feel better, because between you and me"—he shifted his eyes from side to side—"it's probably better that I'm going first, because while I know she will carry on without me, I wouldn't be able to live without her."

I swallowed, but the lump in my throat was persistent. "I think we need a beer," said my father. "Isn't that the manly thing to do?"

I watched his thin back as I followed him into the kitchen, and I tried to imagine what life would be like without him in the world. I couldn't. "Drinking in the daytime is one of the first signs of alcoholism," I said.

He turned around and winked at me. "You only live once." And, for once, I actually felt like a drink.

I went home to Maine and to Poppy, and, to my surprise, Rochelle. For once, I accepted her offer of coffee, and once I got used to the nail polish smell, I found someone who loved Poppy as much as I did, and that was all it took. I put a photograph of them taken at the country fair on my desk at work, and found myself getting lost in thinking about them, the numbers on my desk swimming into nonsense.

The next time I was in my parents' kitchen, he was gone. Mother called the night he died, and I caught the next plane down. Clarrie, tanned and just back from Spain, met me in the airport. I was expecting my mother to still be in her bathrobe, but she was in a somber suit, dark blue rather than black. It wasn't just the suit, however, that made the difference. It didn't look like her. She seemed deflated, like she had collapsed in on herself. Her face was small and pale and frightened. We stood and stared at each other. I hadn't mentioned taxidermy since she had run out that day. She walked up to me and gripped my arms, pinning them to my sides, a look of defiance on her face that crumbled into crying as she said, "Why did the old fool have to die on me?"

I placed my chin on the top of her head and cried into her hair.

Soon the undertaker told us it was time. We composed ourselves a little and walked out into the bright sunlight. I pretended not to notice Wild Ben's truck pull up outside the house.

THIS IS NOT THE GLUTTON CLUB

There was a gray oppressiveness to the air when I got off the train. The damp Yorkshire air was a stark contrast to the sun I had left behind in Bristol. Nevertheless, I felt the moors suited me better. I felt the shackles of my life, of expectations, drop from me as I walked through the station. My uncle's driver awaited me, and I could see he had aged since the last time I saw him. He gave me a curt, deferential nod as I ducked into the back seat of the car and we began the short drive to my uncle's estate.

I had been summoned by letter a month before. The message had been brief—that my uncle desired an audience with me. I filled in the blanks. My uncle, like his driver, was advancing in age, and I, as the favorite nephew of a confirmed bachelor with no children, was his assumed heir. My uncle's sentiments were not one-sided. Although I had not seen him in years, I greatly admired my uncle. He was a man of gravitas and influence who had lived a full and adventurous life. There was a romance to him that was entirely lacking in my staid, traditional but well-meaning father.

I sat in silence as we drove down rain-soaked country lanes edged in dripping hedgerows. I enjoyed the vistas of green fields and heather-purpled moors, still lovely when sodden.

My uncle's estate, Hadesfield, loomed large as we approached the gravel driveway. It was blocky and solidly built of red brick, a controversial choice when most established houses were made of local stone, but my uncle was always one to eschew tradition. The windows reflected the gray atmosphere, like blank eyes. The huge doors swung open to welcome us before we had even made it to the first step. At the sight of Stockton, my uncle's butler, the driver deposited my luggage, nodded again and ran back through the rain to the car.

Stockton smiled at me warmly. "Jonathan," he said. "Young sir has grown. This way. I've prepared your room. Once you are settled, you are to join your uncle for dinner." I thanked him. Stockton had aged too, his hair shot through with white now and his face lined. Yet he still possessed the same wiry energy of old. He picked up my suitcases as if they weighed nothing and sprang up the stairs. My room remained the same. I washed and dressed for dinner.

Once the sun had gone down, the dinner bell rang and I made my way to the dining room. I knew of old that my uncle ate late. He worked in solitude in his study for most of the day and socialized at night. Entering the richly decorated room that had not changed since I was a child, I could barely contain my shock at my uncle's countenance, for it remained as unchanged as the room. He looked as young and as vigorous as the last time I had seen him almost...20 years ago. It was a sharp contrast to the ravages of time I had seen in his staff. I myself had aged, from callow teen to man, and not such a young man at that. My uncle stood well over six feet tall, broad-shouldered and sturdily built—he cut an imposing figure. His dark hair was as full and as lustrous and just a little too long for polite society as it had always been. I could not perceive any hints of snow in it, although the room was dimly lit. Likewise, his beard was as full and as dark as ever. His dark, sharp eyes glinted at me, the edges wrinkling in warmth. This was not the old man on his deathbed that I had imagined. Not the man ready to give up all his worldly possessions as I had supposed. I felt ashamed.

"Jonathan! My boy," he exclaimed and grasped me in a suffocating bear hug. When, at length, he had released me and I had gathered my breath, he gestured to the table. "Come, let's eat. I can't tell you all I have to tell you on an empty stomach."

The cook, as usual, had prepared an excellent meal. One that was simple, in the Yorkshire way, but hearty and filling. My uncle, on the other hand, as I knew from previous visits, had contracted a disease in his expeditions in the tropics and could only eat a restricted diet. Fruits and vegetables were forbidden, as was much else. In fact, the only foodstuff he could seem to ingest were large quantities of red meat and his beloved red wines. Nevertheless, we both ate with gusto and returned to his study afterwards, another glass of wine for him, a brandy for me.

We settled in our places as if I had never been away—my uncle in his large, high-backed armchair near the fire, and I at a lower padded stool at his feet. The years seemed to roll back and once again I felt as when I was a child and young teen, eager to hear of my uncle's travels all over the world and exploits at university, his adventures abroad and in the social scene before I was born. It was a world I had never really known, as confined as I was by my parents and their small world in Bristol. He began to speak.

"Jonathan, I know when I summoned you, you must have thought my number was up and it was time to move in!"

My face reddened, betraying me. I began to splutter a horrified "no" when he cut me off by laughing heartily.

"Of course you did. There's no shame in it. It makes perfect sense. That's not exactly what is going on but I do have something to pass on to you. First, I need to tell you a story, a story that I have never told anyone, a story from before you were born when I was a man even younger than yourself."

The fire roaring, I leaned forward to listen.

"We were young, just out of university, all of us bachelors except one. We were starting in our careers or deciding what kind of living we would like to make. As you know, I never truly decided. The world of industry and commerce were not for me, nor the annals of academia or the corridors of power. A stint in the clergy was, of course, out of the question, although some might argue I would have been a perfect fit. I always had the tremendous good fortune, literally, of never really needing a plan. I had income enough, from my mother's and father's families—a privilege that I hope to pass along to you. Of course, if you decide to continue this clerking business, then I would not deign to stop you." He shook his great head and laughed. "Of course that's not what you want. No one wants to be a bloody clerk—my sister and her damned ideas of respectability.

"But I digress. Some of us knew the women we would like to marry, others were enjoying the search and then others," he gave a rueful smile, "knew that it was never going to be for them. The point is, my boy, that we all felt we were on life's precipice, as it were. It all felt tremendously exciting. Yet, at the same time, I believe we were all quite fearful too. Afeard of not measuring up, afeard of failure, afeard of our lives becoming a frightful bore, so we clung to some of our immature, reckless behavior, some vestige of our youth and university japes. It is this time of our lives that I want to tell you about tonight."

He looked into the fire, and I saw in his expression a sadness, a reflection of his actual age that his physiognomy did not betray.

"There were five of us in all—myself, Tom Langtry and Davy Simmons, who I had roomed with at Oxford; Bertie Young, who I met at the dinner club; and Simon Fetherington, who was married to Davy's sister, Betty. We'd all meet up once a week, the usual things—dinner, drinking, cards, you know, but increasingly we found we all craved a little more excitement. Something to get the blood, or something else, pumping. We visited brothels, but that left poor Simon out of the loop and became too awkward. Between us, I'm sure he would have joined in had he not been paranoid that Davy would go running to tell tales to his sister. Besides, finding good establishments that catered to both mine and their tastes were few. We visited opium dens, visited mediums and tried to contact the dead, table knocking, all sorts of spiritualist nonsense, Ouija boards. We visited insane asylums and prisons. We tried the occult and studied Crowley. But nothing really caught us, nothing hit the spot. Then two events occurred that coalesced into what we had been looking for. First of all, the Glutton Club became the talk of London. You know the one, those chaps from Cambridge who decided they would eat everything they could get their bloody hands on. Nothing too strange or outlandish, nothing too rare for them: gourmands and adventurers they were, and collectors of tastes and experiences. Well, we were very interested in this. You know that the old rivalry stirred up in us. Bertie brought all the information he could get his hands on about them to us.

"Of course, we couldn't do the same thing. We were feckless young men with too much time on our hands, but simple pride would not allow us. We wracked our brains trying to think of what gimmick our little club could have, sat morosely at the gentlemen's club shooting each other's ideas down one after the other. I was all set to run off and become one of the Beast's acolytes when fate intervened.

"I noticed that Roger, our usual waiter, had not been sent to our table. I asked the boy who they had sent instead. 'Where's Roger?'

"He bowed his head and replied, 'He has the flu, sir.'

"'Beg your pardon,'" said Davy, who was a touch deaf from a hunting incident.

"The boy stood straighter and spoke louder. 'I said he has the flu, sir.'

"'Influenza?' I said.

"'Yes, sir.'

"'Is it going around?' said Tom, who barely spoke.

"'I don't know, sir. They just said it was the flu. He's been off work for the past week.' He then asked if we needed anything else. We did not, so he retreated to the kitchen.

"'He'll be lucky if he survives that,' said Davy.

"'Nonsense,' said Bertie. 'I had the influenza once. Took me a fortnight, but I sweated it out. The Turkish baths helped. Roger will be fine.'

"'I'm not sure Roger will have access to Turkish baths,' said Davy.

"'True,' said Bertie, 'and I am possessed with exceptional mental fortitude and an ironclad constitution.'

"We all guffawed.

"'It's true,' he said, reddening. 'I even had whooping cough as a child. I believe I can overcome any illness. All it takes is to be strong in body, but especially in mind.' He tapped his temple.

"'Bollocks,' said Tom, under his breath.

"As you can imagine, the evening moved on, we consumed many more drinks and Bertie still insisted that he could withstand any illness. Why, he could even stand another bout of the flu. If Roger was here right now, he would exhort the man to show him where the miasma emanated whereby he contracted the disease.

"'Isn't it germs? Don't they say it's germs now?' said Simon.

"'And where are germs?' said Davy.

"'On the skin and in the breath, I should imagine,' I said.

"'Well,' said Bertie, 'then I would shake Roger's hand vigorously and have him breathe on me...multiple times!' He continued in the same vein, wobbling on his feet, his face red. Were we cowards for not risking it? Were we not all young? Were we not all hale and hearty? Was it our mental strength we doubted?

"And so, by the end of the night, against everyone's better judgment, Roger's address had been procured from the club manager, and we had clambered into a cab to go and check on the poor man. I have no idea what he thought when five inebriated men he barely knew came thundering to the door of his meager rooms, but he was good enough to let us in despite his obvious ill health. He was too ill to question why we wanted to shake his hand or have him breathe in our faces. He shook his head in confusion when Bertie asked him about miasma, but he took our money gratefully. He went back to bed even more gratefully. Looking back, I wish we had ordered the poor man a doctor. I have no idea whether he lived or died, or whether our nocturnal visit had a detrimental effect on him. I never saw Roger working at the club again.

"Ultimately, two of us contracted the flu: Davy and Simon. Davy took a lot longer to recover than the fortnight that Bertie had mentioned. Simon begged off from any other similar activities. He and his wife were trying for a baby, he said, and he couldn't risk bringing any more sickness into the house. Davy said he understood, he didn't want to get into trouble with his sister any more than Simon did.

"So we were four. Of course, it was Bertie who slapped his hands together and said, 'What malady do you want to try for next?' Our club was thus formed. Not for us the pedestrian act of merely eating, what test was that to the body and brain? No, we would be collectors of experience, but what we would collect was the experience of survival. We would endeavor to catch as many illnesses as we could and live through them. Bertie would start research straightaway. Only Tom murmured dissent, but he was always a patsy for peer pressure, no matter his protestations. We thought about calling ourselves the Malady Club but our competitiveness knew no bounds. We settled on 'Not the Glutton Club.'"

"Wait," I interjected. "You contracted diseases on purpose?"

My uncle chuckled. "Madness, I know, a foolhardy, dangerous enterprise. I won't try and defend it. We were young and foolish and utterly convinced of our own immortality in a way that only the young and foolish truly can be."

"Did you not get very sick?"

"Oh yes, terribly and often. But we seemed to be blessed, you see. We thought it was luck and mental fortitude; but now I am older, I can see now that it was partially those things, yes, but we also had the fortune of being well-fed all our lives, of living comfortably with little worries. All of those things contributed to the very constitution we were so proud of. Some things we were lucky enough not to catch, for they would have surely killed us. Others we caught without even trying. Look here."

My uncle leaned forward and pointed to his cheek.

"Pockmarks, from chickenpox, so damned itchy. I couldn't leave those blisters alone. I'm covered in these damned things. Caught them off a barmaid in Soho." He pulled up his shirt. "Look." His entire torso was studded with scars. "But there's more," he said. He lifted his trouser leg and lifted his calf so it was illuminated by the firelight. I could see that the skin there was pocked in the truest sense. It was stippled and marked in a way I knew only one disease was capable of.

"Smallpox?" I said.

"Yes," he said. "Would you believe it? It wasn't hard to catch, but we had a devil of a time finding someone who had not been inoculated. We were diligent in our quest for infection. We sought out travelers on ships and the wretched from Whitechapel, visited hospitals and Harley Street surgeons, touched skin and blood and all other manner of secretions, drank from vials and syringes and potions. We were idiots."

"Did you suffer other ill effects?"

"I'm fairly sure that I'm sterile from the mumps, but that has never been an issue. I was lucky, for the most part, damned lucky, we all were. Not one of us perished for all our shenanigans, not until the end. Davy had smallpox too, I believe, and a withered leg courtesy of polio. Bertie's poor lungs were shot from tuberculosis, pneumonia, pleurisy, who knows. He had contact with them all. He also went half-daft from syphilis. He didn't mean to catch that, of course. I'm sure his nose would have fallen off, eventually. Tom seemed to fare better than the rest of us. I don't remember him having any lasting effects. Not that it mattered in the end."

"You talk of them as if they are already gone, Uncle."

"I do, don't I? Very astute of you. I speak of them correctly in the past. After all, I am the only one here."

"Did they succumb to illness?"

"In a manner of speaking. Our club lasted, what? Three years, four at the most, a small fraction of our lives, I suppose. We did things that most of polite society would have balked at. We shook hands and embraced with the most diseased of fellows and gals. We ate contaminated food, licked infected objects, sat in the foulest slums, had tea with Typhoid Mary, and we suffered for it. But there is nothing that makes you feel more alive than coming back from the brink of death. It is truly a gift. Believe me when I say, I wouldn't change those years for the world.

"But nothing can stay the same forever. There is no question that our pursuits were taking their toll on our bodies and psyche. My compatriots were starting to turn their attention to their wives and children and establishing themselves in the world. Even I had to mull over what I wanted to do for the rest of my life. Our connection died by degrees rather than a sudden sever. Our meetings became fewer and fewer until we all became nothing but fond acquaintances, an entry on a Christmas card list and nothing more.

"As you know, I spent my time traveling, seeing the world, collecting oddities, making investments, just as I would have liked to see you have done had I not been under strict instructions not to undermine your mother. So the Not the Glutton Club drifted apart. It was over a decade before I saw them again. I was around your age." He leaned back in his chair. In truth, he did not look much older than me, sitting there.

"It began with a very excitable letter from Bertie. Would I be interested in starting up the club again? Perhaps just one more meeting? He had done some research and had found something absolutely extraordinary that he said we would all find fascinating. The tone of his letter was erratic at best, and even the method—the paper was covered in inkblots, and Bertie's once immaculate penmanship was unrecognizable. As it turned out, I was the last to be contacted. The rest of the chaps were on board, and rather gung-ho about it as far as I could tell. I suspected a large part of their interest was middle-age ennui, and as I was experiencing a little myself, I readily agreed. Oh, the foolish things men will do to try to regain their youth!

"Bertie wanted me to host the meeting up here. This place had just been finished. I was surprised. I had assumed that they would be reluctant to leave their beloved South. Bertie said we would require seclusion and I have that in abundance. He asked me to prepare a room for each of them: Bertie, Davy, Tom, and even Simon, who was coming out of retirement for this special meeting. He also asked me to prepare a room for a lady. He assured me that there would be no impropriety. An odd comment; if he knew me at all, he would know that I didn't care. She was part of the research he had to present, he said. I agreed to his terms and we set a date in September. I confess I was more excited at seeing them again than anything to do with the club. My body was getting older and I didn't think I had the stamina to get so sick again."

I looked at my brandy. It was full again. Stockton must have surreptitiously entered and refilled our glasses. I hadn't noticed, riveted as I was to my uncle's story. The study fire was no longer roaring. Now, the bright red coals glowed before they got ready to die.

"Would you believe me if I said it was a dark and stormy night on the moors the night we convened again?" my uncle said. "Well, it was, as if out of the pages of a penny dreadful. The wind outside howled and the moon was a baleful eye looking over us. The rain splattered every windowpane."

>>>≪≪≪

I laughed. "Are you sure, Uncle? This tale has been somewhat fantastical so far without this. Are you spinning me a yarn?"

He looked at me; all mirth vanished from his eyes. "I swear that every word is true, and it is going to get even more fantastical, and I'm going to need you to believe me." He looked into the fireplace.

>>>≪≪≪

"It was good to see my friends again. We were all older, and some of us had worn better than others. Tom appeared the most hale; our little experiments seemed to have barely touched him. Yet the near-silence that he had exhibited in his youth had deepened. He had never married either, and had spent his life cloistered in historical research. He had a case of the nerves, and it bothered me that I had never noticed before. Davy's limp was much more pronounced, and he used a cane. His swollen nose and cheeks were a map of broken red veins. I could smell booze on him from across the room, even before dinner. Simon seemed well enough, but aged too. The worries of family and life itself were written all over him.

"Bertie, though. Bertie was a wreck. As soon as he walked through the door, practically carried by Stockton due to his breathing difficulties, I had significant doubts about the whole enterprise. Bertie was not a man who could afford to get ill. He was mad, syphilis-mad, and I wondered how he had escaped the asylum. It was so bittersweet to see an old friend after so long, but under such diminished circumstances. He said his guest would arrive later. I had Stockton settle him in his room and arranged for everyone to meet at dinner.

"The storm continued unabated as we sat down for our repast. The candles flickered as we ate, affected by draughts that should not have plagued a house so young. Bertie's mysterious guest was announced after dark. I had not seen her. Bertie had escorted her to her room, much to Stockton's consternation. She would not join us for dinner, but we would meet her afterwards.

"I wish I could tell you what we talked of over dinner. I think of it often, wonder over it, try and recall anything I can considering the events that followed, but there is nothing. Banalities, I assume, the awkward exclamations of men who have spent too many years apart and have nothing in common anymore. Too much space and time had occurred for us to ever catch up. We ate, some of us with more enthusiasm than others, and then retired to the very room we are sitting in now."

➤➤➤◄◄◄

My uncle looked around blindly as if, instead of seeing the dying fire, me, our drinks, the furniture, he could see back in time at his friends gathered around him on a stormy night in September many years ago.

➤➤➤◄◄◄

"This room was different then. At Bertie's request, the furniture had been moved to the sides of the room. He insisted that before he introduced his guest, we must all stand in a circle as if we were performing some sort of ritual. The rest of us had looked at each other meaningfully at his commands. It was clear that he was in thrall to his madness, but what were we to do? We humored him and did as he bid.

"Once we had taken our positions, Bertie hobbled into the center of the circle. 'Gentlemen,' he said, 'I hereby convene perhaps the last meeting of the Not the Glutton Club. I came across something, someone, so astonishing, I thought it pertinent to summon you all one last time.' He paused, wobbled a little, his expression becoming grave. 'What you may not know is that I have never given up on our mission. I have spent my life seeking out the rarest of diseases and have held on to my strong constitution and mental fortitude. I have traveled the world, been led down many blind alleyways, but now I believe I have found the ultimate disease carrier. Remember when we took tea with

Mary? A lovely girl, but nothing on who I am going to introduce you to tonight. She is nobility, she is a marvel, and she is indestructible.'

"'Get on with it, Bertie,' said Davy. 'I haven't the legs to be standing here all night while you waffle on.'

"Bertie ignored him. 'May I present to you, Lady Elizabeta Morais.'

"From the darkness at the edges of the room, a lady emerged and stood next to Bertie. She was small and skeletal and her skin was so pale that it appeared lavender in the dim candlelight, shiny and hard, as if she was made more of mineral than flesh. She had long dark hair that spilled down her shoulders like ink and she wore a diaphanous garment in a similar hue to her skin, a simple wrap gown tied at the waist. It was made of sheer cloth and was well beyond anything considered decent at the time. In truth, it was considerably less than what most ladies of the night wore, at least in our acquaintance. It had been a long time since I had been in a house of ill repute, but I remembered enough.

"I watched Simon avert his eyes, but the rest of our party was transfixed. Bertie worried me. His eyes were feverish as he looked upon her. He worked his hands together, rolling one over the other as if trying to hold himself back from reaching out at her.

"'Elizabeta,' said Bertie, licking his lips.

"Elizabeta untied the belt at her waist and shrugged her gown off of her shoulders. It dropped in a puddle on the floor at her feet. I don't believe I was the only one who audibly gasped. She was completely naked. She began to speak; her voice was throaty and low. 'Gentlemen, do not avert your gaze. I came here so you could look upon me.' She turned slowly, facing each of us in turn. 'I am not ashamed,' she said, 'and neither should you be. No shame, no shame.' She looked at us directly in the eyes and said it to each of us. 'No shame. No shame. No shame. Look at my body. Look at what the many years, the many illnesses I have triumphed over have done.' I tore my eyes away from hers and studied her body. It was indeed scarred, horrifically marked and scarred, ravaged by time that was not reflected in her face. She had pockmarks that matched my own, and other marks that I did not recognize. I saw the tell-tale signs of polio and smallpox.

"Bertie spoke. 'I heard a rumor of Elizabeta in a druggist's in Highgate. I knew that I had to find her for one last meeting. I followed her trail. I searched London and Paris. I sent my man to Prague and Budapest. I heard rumors that she was in Bombay and Shanghai. She evaded me for two years, didn't you, my dear?' Elizabeta nodded her head modestly, completely incongruent to her nakedness. 'Finally, I found her. On the edge of the Black Forest of all places! She took some convincing to leave, but I promised that I would reward her handsomely and ensure her passage back to Germany after the meeting. I told her how much it would mean to us to meet her.'

"Elizabeta turned her body again. There were scars on her neck and groin, where cysts or tumors had been. I'd heard the plague presented in those areas of the body, but it couldn't be. I was about to enquire, but she began to speak. 'If you think you see signs of death that surely I should have never been exposed to, never mind survived, then you would be correct.' She laughed.

"Bertie interjected: 'Elizabeta is older than any of us can guess. She has survived more infections than any of us can name.'

"'How?' said Tom.

"Bertie continued. 'By contracting the greatest affliction of all—vampirism!'

"Davy guffawed. 'Come on, Bertie, old chap, all that opium you smoked must have rotted your brain. Vampires are a thing of myth! Everyone knows that. How much has this floozy fleeced you for?'

"'Look at her skin,' said Bertie. 'Is that a natural tone? Look at her scars. How could someone have survived all that without supernatural help?'

"'I dare say you have all survived a few of them, and none of you are bloodsuckers,' said Simon. 'Besides, it's amazing what they can do with paints and whatnot these days.'

"'I believe him,' said Tom quietly. We all twisted our heads towards him. 'Look,' he said. 'That's the Black Death. Those were buboes. They must have burst, drained.' He pointed to Elizabeta's neck. 'When and where did you survive that, Elizabeta?'

"'Vienna, 1679.'

"'Bull,' said Davy, who turned and started to leave but then stopped. He turned back and took his place in the circle. His movements were odd, like he was not in control of his own limbs, like an automaton or a puppet. I soon discovered why. I found too that I could not move of my own volition. I was under some kind of mesmerism. No matter what my mind told my body to do, to move, to protest, to run from the room, it would not obey. It was rooted to the spot as if I were a statue.

"Bertie clapped his hands together. 'Not the Glutton Club, I present one final challenge. We are to be infected with vampirism!' His mouth clapped shut and I could see that he was under the spell too. Elizabeta turned slowly; again she looked at each of us in turn with her glittering eyes."

"Uncle," I interrupted, "surely this really is a tall tale. This cannot be true. Everyone knows that vampires do not exist. I know you to be a rational man. Is this an allegory?"

"Jonathan, I swear on your life that every word of this is true. Have I ever led you astray? Let me get to the end of my tale and all will become clear why I brought you here." He drank deeply from his wine glass.

"Elizabeta stalked over to Bertie. She placed her tiny hands on his face and caressed his cheeks. Then she wrenched his head to one side, showing preternatural strength that belied her emaciated frame. I heard his neck snap. He was dead instantly, dropping to the floor like a stone. She spoke in sepulchral tones: 'Poor Bertie, the madness had gone too far in him. He had to die. Now, who's next?'

"She scanned the room before alighting her eyes on Simon. 'You are a coward, and so full of shame you can barely hold your head up. You would make a terrible vampire. Run, run now and go home. Don't look back, or you'll be given the same fate as Bertie.' Simon visibly unfroze and ran for the door, never looking back. I heard from an acquaintance that he died of heart trouble. His family was there.

"Elizabeta turned her attention to Davy. 'Oh, Davy, Bertie talked a lot about you. Brave and bold, except when it mattered. You never had a backbone either. You called me a floozy and I'm hungry.' She opened her mouth, and I saw her teeth shine in the candlelight. She clamped her mouth down on Davy's neck and drank the lifeblood from him. When he began to drop to the floor, she ripped his throat clean out.

"Tom was next. 'Quiet, nervous Tom,' she said. 'What kind of life have you led? A life of careful tiptoeing. I'm going to make you bold.' She took him in her arms and he cleaved to her. She drained him to the point of death, the color dripping from his face, and then she opened a vein in her own wrist and smashed it into his mouth. I saw the color come back. I saw life come back in his face, but it was not his life. This was a different Tom. I witnessed my own fate. Tom looked at me, looked at his own hands as if seeing them for the first time, and ran off into the night. I have never laid eyes on him since."

"You said you witnessed your own fate?"

"That's precisely what I am telling you. But you interrupt my story again and I am so close to the end."

"Surely, you can't be suggesting—"

>>>—«««

"Elizabeta turned those hypnotic eyes to me. 'Now, you're the adventurer, I know. You're the one who has lived outside the constraints that society would have put on you. Oh, to be a man with money.'

"I felt her teeth on my neck before I even saw her move towards me. As she siphoned away my blood, I saw my life move before my eyes. I saw my mother and father, my beloved nana, your mother, school, university, my time with the club, my travels, Stockton, building this house, and then I felt the hum of nothing. I've never felt peace like it. I suspect I never will again. I was rudely interrupted by the taste of Elizabeta's blood in my mouth. A huge surge rushed through me and that life played back to me in reverse. Elizabeta vanished. I was infected that night, Jonathan. I have been a creature of the night, a vampire ever since."

>>>—«««

He stood and opened his mouth, and yes, I saw the glint of his fangs in the dying firelight.

"You can see I haven't aged, and I won't. You are my heir, and I wanted to give you time to build the life your mother wanted for you—to get married, a career, a family, but what I always suspected is true, isn't it? You're more like me than anyone imagined."

I tried to protest, but why hide the truth? I knew who I was and so did he.

"Come," he said, and opened his arms. "It's time to join the club."

I moved to his embrace and felt the sting of his teeth on my neck.

RISE

It was in June when Janice's shoulder blades began to itch. At first it was a mild prickle; she thought it might be an allergic reaction to the cheap nylon tunic she had to wear for her cleaning job. She'd had to take on extra hours now that Garrett had lost his job at the quarry. It wasn't his fault, he said. He just lost his temper. They were pussies. It was a minor safety violation. Janice nodded. Whenever he started ranting about it, she would go to the window and watch the birds at the bird feeder. She envied the small creatures. They had freedom, the ability to come and go as they pleased. At the same time, she loved them. She loved their wings, their airy bones, their bright eyes and tiny beaks. She even loved the plain ones, with dull brown and gray feathers that didn't shine in the sun. She always made sure that the feeders were full so they didn't have to worry about where to eat. They were so used to her that they flew to the bird table as she stood there.

The itch got worse, even though she'd started wearing a cotton shirt under her tunic. It felt like when you get dry skin in winter, but this was July. After her shower at night, she massaged moisturizer into her skin to try and soothe it, but it didn't make any difference. When Garrett was in bed, she would rub her shoulders against the door frame like a horse at a fencepost. She could swear that she could feel her shoulder blades getting thicker. It made no sense. She didn't tell Garrett. He still hadn't gotten another job and spent his days playing first-person shooter games, sinking further and further into the sofa. She spoke more to the birds at the bird feeder than him.

Through that summer and fall, the itching got worse and her shoulder blades began to swell. The women at work started making cracks about her uniform getting tight. They didn't like her, anyway. They would stand outside and smoke while she carried on working. "How's it going, Janice? Working up a sweat?" one of them would shout, and they would laugh at her.

When she got home, she'd peel off her tunic in the bathroom, sit on the toilet and scratch her shoulder blades in long raking motions. It was oddly satisfying. She'd sit there for over an hour until Garrett shouted and asked what she was doing in there. She'd take a hot shower and feel the sting of the scores she had made. She wore a shirt to bed to hide them. Garrett didn't seem to notice. He hadn't touched her in months.

By October, she couldn't get a tunic over the bulges on her shoulder blades. She got written up for wearing a shirt. She told her boss she couldn't help it. She explained about the lumps. He was the only person she told. Her boss took pity on her and told her that he would order a bigger tunic for her. He knew she needed the money. He asked her why she couldn't see a doctor. Janice shook her head. The health insurance had disappeared with Garrett's job. Her boss told her she could wear her shirt until the new one came in. It was Garrett's shirt, actually. Hers didn't fit anymore. Garrett sneered and told her she must be getting too damn fat.

The women at work stopped with the direct comments but whispered behind their hands. Her posture got funny because she was trying to hide the bulges on her shoulder blades. She wondered if she could bind them somehow but the thought upset her. She didn't want to constrict them. They didn't itch anymore but were very swollen. When she pressed the flat of her palms against them, they didn't feel filled with fluid or solid fat, as she imagined cysts would feel like. They felt springy, filled with something dry and crackling. Janice wondered if she was dying. She couldn't decide if she cared. She really ought to go to the doctor, but what then? Even if she could scrape together the money for an appointment, there was no way she could afford the treatment, whatever it was. Medicine, ointment, or surgery, it was all out of her budget.

She told the birds all about her problems at the bird feeder. She took extra care to give them food now that the weather was getting colder, but something had changed. As she stood there pouring seeds and corn, an overwhelming hunger washed over her. Not for the bird food, but for something else. She finished the job quickly, spilling millet on the ground.

Something was happening with her hands and feet too. They were dry and no matter how much hand or foot cream she put on, they just got scalier. Her toes and fingernails got tougher, stronger. She had a hard time using the nail clippers, until she just gave up. They grew long and yellow, shredding the toes of all her socks.

Garrett continued to sit on the sofa. When she asked him to help out in the house, maybe do a little laundry, cook dinner, he refused. "I'm looking for jobs," he said, but she never saw any evidence of it. "It's not like it's hard work, what you do," he said. "You should have enough energy. You're just lazy." In the past, she would have agreed with him, but something about the thing with her shoulders made her feel removed. She stayed silent. She knew she wasn't lazy. In fact, Garrett was the one who was lazy. Having this thought, something she would have never dared consider before, sent a jolt of excitement up her spine. Maybe one day she would tell him. She'd tell the women at work too.

The weird thing was, whenever she did get tired, or despondent, or just sick of her life, if she touched her swollen shoulder blades, she felt better. It calmed and soothed her, gave her a burst of energy. It made her think that she really could tell all the people in her life what she thought of them. Maybe thank her boss too. Maybe not bother. She could do what she wanted. Maybe. She must be very sick, she thought, perhaps going crazy. She could have tumors, and one was in her brain as well as her shoulders. That would explain it.

She ignored the women at work; what were they to her anyway? She smiled at her boss in the parking lot. He was a little spot of kindness in a largely hostile world. She wondered if she should try and have an affair with him. No. It wasn't what she wanted. She hoped his life was nice. Her new, larger tunic was starting to strain as well. It was the largest they stocked. Soon, she thought, she would have to stay at home, unable to work. She could not hide the hunchback she was becoming. It surprised her that the women at work had not said anything. She was waiting to hear "Quasimodo" as she mopped the floor, but there was nothing. They were silent. Sometimes she saw one of them stare at her with what might have been pity in their eyes. She couldn't ask for another tunic. She would miss her boss, and had no idea how she and Garrett would manage financially. She found she wasn't as worried about this as she thought she would be—probably the tumors.

She started to wear Garrett's sneakers; her own didn't fit her anymore, her toenails too long and tough to fit in them. He didn't leave the house, so he never noticed. She supposed that she could wear sandals, but she saw how people recoiled at her hands, especially at the store when she paid for groceries, got Garrett's beer, and she couldn't take the extra stares. She began to wear cotton gloves, two sizes too big. When an old lady stared at those too, Janice lost her temper and snarled, "What are you looking at?" The old woman backed away, fear in her eyes.

That evening, she noticed the birds pecking around the bird table. She had been neglecting them. Overcome with remorse, she carried the seeds over. Again, that hunger. This time she could not resist. She clamped a scaly hand on one of the small brown birds, snatched it and stuffed it in her mouth. Choking on the feathers, she crunched down on the tiny bones. The rest of the birds flew away. Janice placed her birdfeeder and seeds on a neighbor's doorstep. She walked back to the trailer, blinded by tears.

Garrett finally noticed one night when she was cooking dinner. She stood at the oven, opening it to see if the meatloaf was cooked when he walked in. "Janice, what the hell is wrong with your back?"

What could she say? "It's not my back, it's my shoulder blades. I'm fine," she said, even though she wasn't. The skin was starting to split, lesions forming and long stretch marks down the length of her back.

"Take the shirt off," said Garrett. "Let me have a look." So she did. He gasped when he saw them and then looked her in the eyes for the first time in months. What was it she could see in his eyes? Love? Pity?

Perhaps both. An immediate change shimmered over him, like he was possessed. "I'll finish dinner, Janice." He helped her put the shirt back on. He put his hands gently on her upper arms and guided her into the lounge. She sat down on the sofa in his usual spot. "Take the day off tomorrow, Janice. In fact, take the week off. We'll get you to the doctor."

It was much too late. Janice found she was boiling with anger. If he could do these things for her, if he could be so nice, then why hadn't he been? She wanted to tell him to fuck right off, scream in his face. Ask him how he could have been such a dick all these years when he had the capacity to be so nice, so helpful. She'd had no idea that this version of Garrett was inside him. She could barely look at him.

She again took refuge in the bathroom. She peeled off her gloves and took off his shoes. She undressed completely and stood at the mirror, turning slowly. Janice studied her reflection. She took in her sagging breasts and humped back, she looked at her soft belly and hips, she examined the claws on her hands and feet, and she didn't feel ashamed for the first time in her life. This was her, and it was okay. On this epiphany, she felt a searing pain in her shoulder blades that caused her to gasp and then scream. The skin on her lumps was tearing open and whatever was inside was escaping. Hearing the noise, Garrett hammered on the thin, hollow wood of the door, busted open the lock and crashed into the bathroom to witness her transformation.

Janice doubled over in pain as two enormous feathered wings emerged from her back and unfurled in the dingy bathroom, filling the entire cramped space. Janice looked in the mirror again, the physical pressure and pain gone. She flexed her iron-gray wings and fluttered them tentatively. Maneuvering them was as easy as breathing. She looked over at Garrett. He had dropped to his knees and was praying to a god he had claimed never to believe in. She pitied him, but not much. She thought about how she could kill him. How, with a single swipe of a claw, she could take out his throat. She didn't, though. She left him there on the scarred linoleum floor. She flapped her wings, a whirlwind in that tiny bathroom, knocking over shampoo bottles, ripping out the shower curtain. She began to rise, her feet lifting off the ground. Controlled and powerful, she broke through the ceiling and roof as if it was nothing, splintering the wood. She took to the skies. There was no limit now.

PUBLICATION HISTORY

"The Limbo Lounge" original to this collection

"Porch" original to this collection

"Ghost Maker" © 2017, originally published in *Wicked Haunted*

"Sermon from New London" © 2018, originally performed on *Toasted Cake #198*

"St. Scholastica's Home for Children of the Sea" © 2019, originally published in *Wicked Weird*

"Crab" original to this collection

"Black Shuck Tavern" original to this collection

"The Last Witch in Florida" original to this collection

"Cellar Door" original to this collection

"Whitechapel" original to this collection

"The Tale of Bobby Red Eyes" © 2018, originally published in *New England Speculative Writers Preview Stories*

"Devour" © 2018, originally published in *The Muse and the Flame*

"Infection" original to this collection

"Janine" original to this collection. The blue devils in this story are based on an original concept by Thomas Washburn Jr.

"Surviving my Parents" original to this collection

"This Is Not the Glutton Club" original to this collection

"Rise" original to this collection

ACKNOWLEDGMENTS

Acknowledgements are scary in themselves. The terror is that you will forget someone. I know I will and it will be too late, so if you think you should be in here and you aren't, you're right. Thank you.

A huge thank you to Trepidatio Publishing, without whom this book would not exist. Thank you to my editors, Scarlett R. Algee and Sean Leonard, and to Don Noble for my cover with a skull on it.

Thank you to my writing group, the Tuesday Mayhem Club: Peter Dudar, Morgan Sylvia and April Hawkes. Your unwavering support and care has been essential. I couldn't have done this without you. Thank you to all the editors who took a chance on my stories: Tina Connolly, Amber Fallon, Cara Flannery, Scott T. Goudsward, Daniel G. Keohane, and David Price. Thank you to Thomas Washburn Jr for the blue devils.

I am incredibly lucky to have the colleagues I have at Topsham Public Library. Not only do they make it a great place to go to every day, but they are some are my biggest supporters and readers. Thank you, all of you.

To my family, my mum, and my brothers and sisters. Thank you for just rolling with whatever weird thing I wanted to do next and being proud of me anyway.

For those who have helped me make the big and little steps in this writing business: Stephanie Doyon, Mary Rickert, Catherynne Valente, Heath Miller, and Michelle Renee Lane, and to the wider horror and weird fiction community who, without exception, have been warm and welcoming and kind and funny—thank you for making me feel so at home.

And finally, Steve, who holds me, our life and everything together, and Odin, Mothra and Grim, who make life worth living.

ABOUT THE AUTHOR

Emma J. Gibbon is a horror writer, speculative poet and librarian. Her stories have appeared in various anthologies including *Wicked Weird*, *Wicked Haunted*, and *The Muse & the Flame* and on the *Toasted Cake* podcast. She also has a story upcoming in *Would but Time Await: An Anthology of New England Folk Horror* from Haverhill Publishing. This year, she has been nominated twice for the Rhysling Award for her poems "Fune-RL" (*Strange Horizons*) and "Consumption" (*Eye to the Telescope*). Her poetry has also been published in *Liminality*, *Pedestal Magazine* and is upcoming in *Kaleidotrope*. Emma is originally from Yorkshire and now lives in Maine in a spooky little house in the woods with her husband, Steve, and three exceptional animals: Odin, Mothra, and M. Bison (also known as Grim). She is a member of the New England Horror Writers, the Science Fiction & Fantasy Poetry

Association, the Angela Carter Society, and the Tuesday Mayhem Society. Her website is emmajgibbon.com.

Printed in the USA
CPSIA information can be obtained
at www.ICGtesting.com
LVHW090309061023
760130LV00004B/607